Spiderweb for Two

A Melendy Maze

Spiderweb for Two

A Melendy Maze

WRITTEN AND ILLUSTRATED BY

ELIZABETH ENRIGHT

A YEARLING BOOK

Published by
Dell Publishing Co., Inc.
1 Dag Hammarskjold Plaza
New York, New York 10017

Yearling ® TM 913705, Dell Publishing Co., Inc.

ISBN: 0-440-48203-8

Reprinted by arrangement with Henry Holt And Company, Inc.

Printed in the United States of America

One Previous Edition

August 1987

10 9 8 7 6 5 4 3 2 1

CW

FOR ROBIN GILLHAM

CONTENTS

Spiderweb for Two

A Melendy Maze

CHAPTER I

The Shadow's Peak

RANDY WAS certain that this was going to be the worst winter of her life. She said so to Cuffy.

"Cuffy, this is going to be the worst winter of my life," she said.

"Well, if that's the way you've planned it, I guess that's the way it'll be," said Cuffy, who was ironing (the whole kitchen smelled warm and scorchy); then she looked at Randy and relented a little. "I know it's pretty hard on you when you're used to having 'em all here. The house seems awful lonesome I'll admit; but there's school and a lot of things to do, and it's not as if you was *all* alone. There's still Oliver."

"Oh, Oliver!" said Randy in a tone of withering scorn, glaring at her youngest brother. "All he's interested in is his old planes and his old bugs and his old guns; *he's* no fun."

Oliver was stung. "Who says *you're* such a bargain?" he inquired.

"Now that will be enough of that," said Cuffy firmly, setting the iron down with a warm thud. "If you're going to commence bickering and insulting each other the winter will be a bad one for certain sure."

"She's been a pain in the neck ever since Sunday when they left," complained Oliver. Since this was only Monday afternoon Randy did not feel that she had been a pain in the neck for an unreasonable length of time, but she disdained to argue. Giving her brother a look which signified disgust not only with him but with the entire world, she left the room.

The house was sadly quiet; she was not used to it like that. She was used to plenty of racket and commotion, for the Melendys were a large family whose favorite activities included music, drama, dancing and arguing, none of which is silently accomplished. Today there were no sounds at all; not even the typewriter peckings from Father's study. Father was away. As usual, thought Randy bitterly. Why can't he *ever* stay home and just write, the way he used to? Why doesn't he care anything about his family? But this thought was so manifestly unjust, so outrageous, in fact, that she felt slightly better for the moment and started to sing as she went upstairs. She knew as well as anybody else that part of the way her father managed to support his family was by lecturing at various universities. But today she was not interested in justice; she was more interested in sorrow. Why can't he run a little store in Carthage, or print a newspaper, or work in a bank, like other people's fathers, thought Randy, and stopped singing.

In the upstairs hall she hesitated for a moment and then went into her brother Rush's room. It was as empty and as silent as the rest of the house; only a sleepy fly buzzed at the pane; and it was tidy, Randy had never seen it so tidy before. The only untidy thing about it was Isaac, Rush's dog, who was lying in the armchair where he was never supposed to be because he always had fleas and was always shedding. He rolled a guilty eye like a wet licorice drop at Randy, but she only patted his head.

"Stay where you are," she told him. "Poor thing, you'll have a long wait; it's weeks and weeks just till Thanksgiving, and after that it's weeks till Christmas. You just stay there and enjoy yourself. I won't tell Cuffy."

Though Isaac was really Rush's dog, he was loved devotedly by all. John Doe, the other dog, was loved too, though it was generally conceded that he had less character and personal charm than Isaac. He also had less heart; instead of mourning for the absent he was at this minute in the kitchen, Randy knew, uttering low growls of pleading, and watching for Cuffy to open the icebox door.

Randy drifted about the room touching the books, the boxing gloves, the music scores. She took a look into the closet, even, but it depressed her. It was so unnaturally neat: the shirts hung upon hangers, the shoes in pairs against the wall instead of upside down and on their sides all over the floor, leading their own independent lives the way they usually did.

"And it will probably always look like this, now, even when he's home," mourned Randy. "They teach them to be neat at boarding school."

She sighed deeply, patted Isaac again, and departed from the room, leaving the door open so Isaac could come and go.

Next she went into her elder sister Mona's room. This was not quite such a shock, for Mona was a fairly tidy girl, and the room did not look so very different from the way it did when she was at home. Still it *was* different; it couldn't fool Randy. Mona was the actress of the family, and a real actress at that; for several winters, now, she had played the young girl's part in a radio program that was broadcast from a city station, and this year it had been decided that she should go to school in the city as well, since it would save travel to and fro. She was staying with the Melendys' beloved friend, Mrs. Oliphant, an independent old lady with an extra bedroom and a great fondness for children: particularly the Melendy children.

Randy went to the ruffled dressing table which Mona had decorated herself, using an old organdy party dress to make the ruffle; if you knew where to look, you could still find the large turnip-shaped inkstain which had caused the end of its career as a party dress. On top of the table was a collection of little perfume bottles; Mona was proud of these and did not like anyone to meddle with them, but after all she was away. Randy unstoppered first one bottle and then the next, pressing each against her nose in turn; from every one she dabbed a little perfume on her wishbone. Afterward she wished she hadn't; she couldn't smell the plain air any more, a great rosette of fancy scents seemed fastened to the end of her nose, and did not in any way make her feel better.

She leaned down and looked into the little triple mirror on the dressing table; three gloomy selves looked back.

"Ugly thing," she said, scowling. "Hideous old mule-face."

Actually she was not ugly at all, and when she thought about it, did not usually consider herself so; it was the feeling behind the face that she addressed. She was not often in such a bad mood, and had rarely in her life had a chance to be lonesome. Now she was both. And goodness knows when I'll stop feeling this way, she lamented to herself; first they'll all be away at school for years, and then they'll be away at college for years, and then, gosh, I suppose they'll all get *married!*

She went out of Mona's room still wrapped in a cloud of mixed perfumes and, deciding to do the thing thoroughly, went up the stairs through the Office (which was what the Melendys called their playroom) and up yet another short, steep flight to the cupola at the very top of the house. This was the personal domain of the Melendys' adopted brother, Mark, who had gone away to school with Rush. The cupola was a small, light room, really a sort of little cabin on the roof, with a window in each wall for each direction: one apiece for East, West, North and South. Randy chose the North window to press her nose against, as that presented the gloomiest view. It seemed suitable to her that the weather was unfriendly: not raining, but about to rain; grey, sullen, with all the color gone from everything; even the grass looked grey, and the old, tall Norway spruces that guarded the house seemed black and shabby, like monstrous molting crows.

"This is the way it will always be, every day when I come home from school from now on," said Randy unreasonably, and as she looked north toward the town of Carthage, the view suddenly buckled and divided before her eyes as first one, and then another, large tear swelled and wabbled and rolled down her cheek.

It was a long time since she had cried, and she made the most of it. Afterward she felt better. She wiped her eyes on the edge of Mark's bedspread and still hiccupping faintly went down the steep little stairs. Oliver was sitting on the floor of the Office. There were four chairs, a couch, and a piano stool in the Office, but Oliver preferred the floor.

He looked rather awed. "You've been crying," he said.

"I know it," said Randy.

"I heard you but I didn't think I should interrupt," Oliver said; he stood up. "Don't feel so bad, Randy. It's going to be okay, prob'ly. I feel lonesome, too, kind of, but it's going to be okay."

"I suppose you do feel lonesome, don't you?" said Randy, who had not considered this before. She patted his shoulder blade. "You're a nice boy. I ought to appreciate you more."

"You appreciate me enough," Oliver said.

"Let's ask Cuffy for something to eat," Randy suggested. "Crying always makes me hungry."

They clattered down the stairs, and the cheerful noise brought Isaac out of Rush's room; he went down the next flight with them, barking sociably all the way.

"Lands," said Cuffy, as they all exploded into the kitchen, and John Doe raised his voice in greeting. "I thought less young ones around would mean less noise, but it don't seem to work out like that. Here, now, I made a cake right after lunch, and I kept the frosting bowl for you to lick. I didn't want to give it to you before; and there's two bones in the icebox for the dogs.

Better give them to 'em now, Oliver, so's we can have some peace."

Randy hugged Cuffy's familiar waist—or what would have been a waist on a thinner person; it was thick, warm, solid, and creaked faintly when she moved, for Cuffy wore strong, old-fashioned corsets. Everything about her—the creaking, the gentle scolding, the kind, preoccupied face—contributed to the Melendy children's conviction that their home was the coziest, pleasantest place in the world.

Luckily Cuffy had made a fudge cake, as fudge frosting certainly provides the best bowl-licking. Randy and Oliver chipped and scraped with two big spoons, their faces happy and absorbed and every grief forgotten.

"Now clear out and see if there's any mail, why don't you?" said Cuffy when the bowl was completely polished.

"It's too soon to hear from any of them yet," said Randy.

"Nevertheless, there just might be a letter, and I want to mop this kitchen. And take those two beasts with you."

Oliver and Randy and the dogs departed by the back door. The day was very grey and still; leaves dropped from trees because their stems had failed them; there was no wind. They came down sadly, idly, through the air. Randy walked slowly, and Oliver dawdled a little way behind her, stopping now and then to look at a bug, to throw a pebble. Isaac and John Doe were of a different frame of mind; they sniffed, zigzagged, cavorted; being alive and out of doors were enough to make them happy.

"In the mailbox," predicted Randy, "there will be bills and nothing else."

"No, not today," said Oliver, who was a practical boy. "It's not the first of the month, and it's not the middle."

"All right, so then there'll just be post cards advertising sales of dishpans and men's shoes and other dull things," said Randy, determined to look on the dark side as long as possible.

The mailbox appeared the same as usual; its flag alert, its mouth closed. When they opened it they found three things inside: a letter for Cuffy from her cousin Mrs. Theobald, a postal card advertising—oddly enough—a sale of men's shoes, and a medium-sized envelope addressed in unfamiliar handwriting to:

Miss Miranda Melendy
and
Master Oliver Melendy

"Heaven's sake!" said Randy. "Who could it be from? It's not any of their writing or writings, or however you say it."

"It looks like a grownup's writing," Oliver decided. "Where's it from?"

"The postmark says New York: September twelfth,

eleven A.M., it says. That could be anybody; we know thousands of people in New York."

"Well, for Pete's sake, open it!" said Oliver, who preferred facts to mysteries any day.

Randy tore open the envelope; inside it was a sheet of matching blue paper on which a poem was written. She read it aloud to Oliver:

> "I point a clue for you to find,
>   But find me first. Near by I stand.
> Among the tallest of my kind,
>   At four o'clock on a fine day
>   My shadow's peak lies on the land
>   Where, if you spade the earth away,
>   A golden clue will come to hand
>   And speed you on the perilous way!"

Underneath, at the bottom of the page a note was added. "P.S." (it said). "This clue must be uncovered before many days have elapsed. The sun changes each day, so—where my shadow falls this week, that is the spot where you must seek! And not a word to anyone!"

Randy and Oliver were both astounded.

"Now who on earth?" said Randy.

"And what are they talking about?" said Oliver.

"Well, a search I guess. Some kind of a search for something or other, but I wonder what?"

"I wonder why?" said Oliver.

"I wonder who?" said Randy.

Neither one looked sad or thoughtful any longer. They were as alert and interested as Isaac or John Doe, picking up a new scent.

"It says the *perilous* way," Randy pointed out with pleasure.

"Maybe there's booby traps along the way and some kind of a bomb at the end of it," suggested Oliver, positively glowing.

"Oh, I don't think it's likely, do you? I hope it's not some horrid kind of joke with snakes and rats or anything, though."

"Who'd play a joke like that on us? No one hates us, do they?"

"Not that I know of, but you never can tell. I think it all sounds friendly, though. Let's start to hunt. 'Near by I stand. Among the tallest of my kind . . .' What could that be, I wonder? A person? Willy Sloper, maybe?"

"Oh, fine! I suppose Willy's just going to stand in the same place every day at four o'clock and let his shadow fall where the clue is buried! Oh, sure!"

"No, I guess it's a Thing and not a Person. And if it's a Thing, it's probably a tree."

"That's what I think, too. Rush's oak, maybe?"

"It's certainly the tallest one around. Come on, let's go!"

The oak tree of which they spoke stood high in the woods. Among its lower boughs their brother Rush had built a tree house which still was perched there, holding a drift of leaves and acorns, and providing a fine veranda for squirrels and blue jays.

Randy and Oliver and John Doe and Isaac came bursting through the underbrush, scratched with brambles and stuck with burrs.

"If only the sun was out!" said Oliver.

"But it's too late, anyway; it must be after five."

"If the sun *was* shining, and it *was* four o'clock the top of the shadow would be about up here, I bet."

"Oh, no, never, that's too near. It would be way-up-about-here," insisted Randy, tearing her way through briars and wild clematis to a point higher up the hillside.

"But Randy, listen! If the sun was out, you know something? I bet there wouldn't be any shadow up here; at least not a separate one that you could see. There'd be just a big mess of all kinds of shadows because there's such a lot of trees around."

Randy looked at him respectfully. "I bet you're right. And anyway who says it has to be an oak?"

"No. It could be one of the tulip trees—gosh, they're *all* tall—or a sycamore, or a birch, or an elm, or a pine——"

"Goodness, then we'll never find it. There are about a hundred thousand trees around this place."

She and Oliver turned and started down the slope. The woods were loud with woodpeckers and jays. Randy paused. "I've thought of something. Listen, it says here 'my shadow's peak'! Are we ever dumb! Does an oak tree's shadow fall in a peak? Or an elm tree's, either?"

"The Norway spruces!" shouted Oliver. "The two by the house! The thing said it stood near by!"

They were running now; galloping down through the woods with the dogs plunging beside them.

Beside the house, funereal, solemn as ever, stood the two tall guardian trees. They had been there, guarding and growing, for nearly a century; and the Melendys themselves had climbed their prickled branches, hidden in their shade, listened to their windy sighing for years, without once noticing that the tree closest to the house was the least bit taller than its brother. They noticed it now.

"That must be the one!" cried Randy.

"Brother, it's a big tree!" said Oliver, rapidly walking backward across the lawn. "The top of its shadow would fall about here, I bet."

"Oh, no, *much* farther back," said Randy, disagreeing again. Oliver was bending forward now and prowling, examining the ground. If he had had a magnifying glass, he would have looked like Sherlock Holmes. He did have a stick, and from time to time he prodded in the grass with it.

"No fair digging till the sun comes out," said Randy sternly. "We must do this thing Right. We must obey the Rules. Tomorrow at four o'clock we'll start the search."

But the next day it rained. The day after that was grey and cloudy. On the next the sun was brilliant until half past three when great clouds smoked up into the sky and shed an unseasonable thundershower. The next day it rained again.

"My soul and body!" cried Cuffy, her patience frayed at last. "I never saw you young ones fret about the weather so before. I never saw *any* young ones carry on like that about it. A little rain. A little damp. You'd think you was sixty-five years old, the pair of you, with the arthritis and the gout and the rheumatism and chronic sinus trouble besides. Go on up to the Office now. *Play* something."

"I can't keep my mind on anything, can you?" said Randy, as they trudged up the two flights of stairs. "All I can do is hate the weather."

"It just better clear up quick," said Oliver threateningly. "The week's about over."

They killed what was left of the afternoon by playing a game of parcheesi which never reached an end; they were each playing with two sets of men, and as the game was constantly interrupted by trips to the window to look at the weather (which showed them nothing but bad news), they never could be sure whose turn it was to play and spent a great deal of the afternoon in argument.

Several times during the night Randy got out of bed to look out the window: the sky was ominously dark without a spark of stars; but when she woke up, she knew, even before her eyes were open, that the morning was fair.

She and Oliver were not at their best in school that day: every time a cloud darkened the classroom Randy forgot the answer to any question she was asked, and Oliver misspelled his own name twice.

But at last school was over. Willy Sloper called for them in the old station wagon Mrs. Oliphant had given them long ago, which was always elegantly called the Motor—and the sun stayed out.

"Randy," said Oliver suddenly, shouting above the spasmodic burst of the exhaust and the merry clatter of loose windows, "Randy! What if it isn't the spruce tree after all?"

Randy looked at him fiercely. "Of course it is. It has to be!" she said; but apparently she was not so certain as she sounded, for in a minute she added, "What if it's not a tree at all? Maybe it's the steeple of a church."

They were so quiet after that that Willy turned to look at them.

"You kids okay?" he asked.

"Well, yes and no," said Randy.

"We've got worries," Oliver explained.

"Anything I could do to help?"

"We're sworn to secrecy," Randy said darkly. "Or we'd have asked you to help us days ago."

They continued in silence (except, of course, for the wild coughing pandemonium of the Motor) and when they got home, they had the greatest trouble evading Cuffy, who seemed to have a lot of ideas about things she thought they ought to do, and wished to know, pressingly, why they needed to take two of her big cooking spoons out of the kitchen.

"Oh, just for something," said Oliver airily. "Just for something we have to do."

"We'll bring them right back, Cuffy dear," said Randy, smiling brilliantly; then they danced out of the kitchen, ran out of doors, doubled back around the house and crept up on the spruce trees.

Just in time, too. The hour was exactly four; and they saw at once that the shadows of the two trees lay long and pointed, in peaks; one just a little longer than the other.

As they began to dig up the grass and earth, Oliver had another gloomy thought. "Maybe spoons won't be the thing to dig with," he said. "It might be buried deep: six feet deep, or nine, or ten. Maybe we need a spade."

"Maybe we need a steam shovel," said Randy. "Oliver, you're a pessimist."

They went on digging: struck something, shrieked with excitement, found that it was a stone, went on digging. Randy's spoon struck something else.

"It's it! It's it!" she screamed joyfully, and she and Oliver together uncovered a small tin box, somewhat rusted.

"Wouldn't call it gold," said Oliver; but when they opened it they found, wrapped in a piece of paper, a walnut made of golden metal, and this also was a little box. Inside it was a folded piece of paper—the same blue paper on which the first clue had been written.

Her fingers clumsy with excitement, Randy smoothed out the paper on her knee and read aloud the message it contained:

"Call and I will be close to you,
    As I am close to that kind heart
Which loves you well, though knowing not the part
It plays in bringing you the second clue."

Oliver and Randy looked at each other.

"Call what?" said Oliver.

"Call who?" said Randy. "You can't just *call*."

"Well, let's see. . . . It says something about a kind heart that loves us well."

"Of course that's Cuffy," said Randy.

"But it could be Father, you know. Or maybe it could be Willy."

"I don't think they mean Father," Randy said. "Because it says call and I'll be close to you, and Father's about fifteen hundred miles away in Minneapolis, so it doesn't make any sense."

"I don't know, though. He could fly. If we called him by telephone and said we needed him, I mean. Then he'd be close to us."

"I don't think they'd advise anything so expensive, do you? Jeepers, I hope they wouldn't. We'd better try the kind hearts around here first."

CHAPTER II

A Loving Heart

Call and I will be close to you,
  As I am close to that kind heart
  Which loves you well, though knowing not the part
It plays in bringing you the second clue.

CUFFY HAD snatched a few moments for herself. She
was sitting in the kitchen rocker reading an article
on water-color painting. She did not know why she was
reading it, she had never painted a water color in her life
and had no wish to do so, either, but she found it sooth-

ing to read about, for some reason. Too soothing, finally. The rocking chair chirped and thudded, chirped and thudded, slowly and more slowly, until at last it stopped. Cuffy's head rested against the back of her chair, her mouth fell open, and gentle sounds of sleep issued from it to mingle with the other peaceful sounds made by the marching clock, and the occasional thumping of John Doe's hind leg as he scratched away at his own personal fleas. (Isaac, of course, was upstairs in Rush's armchair, scratching away at his.)

Cuffy did not hear Randy and Oliver as they tiptoed in and stood before her.

"She looks nice, doesn't she?" whispered Randy. "Peaceful and nice. I hardly ever saw Cuffy asleep in my whole life before."

"She's a beautiful woman," said Oliver seriously. He meant it, too. For though Cuffy was elderly and stout and wore bifocal glasses and false teeth, there was that in the way she was and the way she spoke that caused him to think of her as beautiful.

"Where could it be, do you think? In her pocket?" said Randy. "She always has a lot of things in her pockets."

"She doesn't know she's got it, remember," whispered Oliver.

They stood staring at her speculatively. John Doe got up reluctantly from under the kitchen table and came over to them slowly, pretending to be a very old tired dog, and sniffed at their shoes. It was a wasted effort; the shoes carried just the usual outdoor smells: grass, leaves, earth, nothing new. He went back to his place and lay down, letting his bones thump with boredom. The clock trudged on.

"Should we wake her up?" whispered Oliver.

"No, let her sleep. We'll come back later."

But at that moment the big, glossy magazine slid the last of the way down Cuffy's sloping lap and crashed onto the floor. Cuffy's mouth closed with a snap, her eyes flew open, and she found herself confronted by two staring children.

"Well, what's the matter?" demanded Cuffy uneasily, sitting up. "Did I talk in my sleep, or what?"

"No, we were just watching you," said Oliver.

Nobody likes to be watched while he sleeps, it seems an invasion of his privacy. Cuffy did not care for it any more than the next one.

"Well, if a person can't just drop off without drawing a crowd, it's too bad," she remarked, in some annoyance.

"We thought you looked nice. Oliver said you looked beautiful," Randy told her. Cuffy scoffed at that, but it made her feel better all the same, and she was rather pleased, too, when Oliver, big boy though he was, climbed into her lap. The chair resumed its rocking, and Cuffy began to sing:

"Mr. Froggy he did ride, and a-hum
    Mr. Froggy he did ride,

Sword and pistol by his side,
And a-hum and a-hum and a-hum.
He rode till he came to a big white hall . . .

"Remember when I used to sing you that?" asked Cuffy tenderly. "Every night while you was teething; you wouldn't stand for any other song only just that one, and—here! Oliver. What are you looking for in my pockets?"

"I'm frisking you, Cuff," said Oliver gleefully, and opened his hand to show what he had found: two elastic bands, a little nest of string, a wad of name tapes saying Rush Melendy, and a soda mint tablet.

"Well, of all the—— Randy! What in the world! You too?"

Randy, having frisked the other pocket, displayed a handkerchief, a couple of hairpins, a leaf of rose geranium, and a folded paper. She opened it eagerly.

"Hooray! There's writing on it!"

"Read it! Read it!" yelled Oliver.

"Tell Willy fix pipe Mr. M's bath," read Randy. "Tell tack upstairs carpet *down*. Oliver milk of mag? 1 doz. oranges. 10 lbs. pots. Clorox. Fleasoap. Write Coral."

"Maybe there's something *to* it," suggested Oliver guardedly. "A riddle kind of hidden away. Code, or something."

"If you ask me it's you two who're talking in riddles," said Cuffy indignantly. "And it's downright rude to rifle folk's pockets and read their private lists like that. Downright rude."

"Aw, we're sorry, Cuff," said Oliver. "We had to do it. It's like a—like an order, sort of, only we can't explain."

"We're just looking for something," Randy said.

"Looking for *what*, in heaven's name?"

"We don't even know."

"Don't *know*? Don't know what you're *looking* for?"

"That's all we can tell you, Cuffy," said Randy. "We're sworn to secrecy."

"The amount of mystery you young ones can cook up, the amount of secrets—" said Cuffy. "All you children seem to thrive on secrets; seem to need 'em like you need vitamins in the diet. All right, if you can't tell me what you're after, there's no way I can help you, is there now? So get off my lap, Oliver. I've got things to do."

"No, wait a minute, Cuffy," said Oliver. "This pin you always wear—I never saw you *not* wear it—was it a locket once, by any chance? Does it open?"

Cuffy looked down at the old cameo brooch at the neck of her dress. It was set in a frame of gold and carved on it was the profile of a Greek lady wearing grapes in her hair and a dove on her shoulder. The Melendy children knew the brooch by heart, knew every grape and every tendril, every feather on the dove; but no one had ever thought before that it might be a locket.

"It's funny none of you ever asked me that before," said Cuffy, fumbling at the catch and unfastening the pin. "Because yes, Oliver, it was a locket once; see here's the hinge, and look, it opens still, like this."

The cameo flew open like a tiny oval door, but instead of a folded slip of blue writing paper the children, disappointed at first, saw the faded photograph of a child: a small, serious face framed in a mass of long curling hair.

"Who is that girl?" demanded Oliver, somewhat indignantly. "You never showed me that before!"

Cuffy smiled teasingly. "Other folks have secrets too, you know."

"No, but honestly, Cuffy, who is it?" wheedled Randy.

"I'll tell you," said Cuffy. "Don't know why I never have told anyone; I kind of kept it to myself all this long, long time. Oliver, fetch my mending basket, will you? And Randy if you could find my glasses . . ."

Randy and Oliver felt surprised, a little put out, that Cuffy had *any* secrets they didn't know about. They had been so certain they knew everything about her: all about her family, the farm she'd been raised on, her school days (even the names of her favorite teachers), the man she would have married if he hadn't been killed, the man she finally did marry and live with happily for thirty years (Eustace W. Cuthbert-Stanley) until his death, and about their house in Massachusetts, and any number of other things. . . . It came as a shock that

all these years the long-nosed cameo lady had been concealing something from them. But they—all the Melendys—had more than their normal share of curiosity;
they burned for answers always. Having located and
brought both mending basket and spectacles, Oliver lay
down on the linoleum beside John Doe, and Randy sat
up on the kitchen counter with the coffee canister in her
lap. From time to time she opened it and drew in its
fragrance with long, loud pleasurable sniffs.

"Okay, go on, tell," commanded Oliver.

"Just wait, now, wai—t, till I get my needle
threaded. . . . The blame eye keeps jumping away
from me. There now, caughtcha!" Cuffy drew the long
thread through, located a burst heel in one of Oliver's
socks and began her story.

"You know about the farm that I was raised
on. . . ."

"In Kneeland Center, Wisconsin," supplied Oliver. "A hundred and forty-seven acres, pasture and
woodland; ten miles from Indian Rocks, and right on
the Sac River——"

"Have I said it all that often?" But Cuffy loved to
describe the happy background of her childhood, and
continued inexorably to describe it again, in spite of
Randy's pointed sighs into the canister.

"Yes, right on the river, it was, or part of it, and
it was lovely land, just lovely. Good rich soil. Wonderful
crops we always had, and our cows gave the most milk of
any around. Clover! Well, you never saw clover-tops so

big; big as plums, about, and the corn grew high as houses; almost as high. My father, he hardly ever stopped his work a minute and my mother was the same, and the place showed it; and us children showed it too, I don't mind saying. We did our chores without asking questions and we minded our manners, too. We wasn't always putting off and searching for excuses——" Cuffy looked sternly at her audience, through the upper half of her bifocal lenses.

"Now, Cuffy," said Randy uneasily. "Times have changed. We're products of another era."

"We-ell," Cuffy hesitated on the brink of a lecture, but Oliver forestalled her and returned her to the path of narrative by asking a judicious question. (Though he knew the answer well.)

"Let's see, how many children were there, now?"

"Four of us at the time I'm telling about. Quintus wasn't born till two years later. There was my older sister Marcella and my brother Homer and the baby, Albert Edward. We all had our chores—a lot of them, too—but we had plenty of playtime, besides, and it was a wonderful place for children——"

Cuffy laid her sewing in her lap and smiled at her memory of the distant place.

"There was a hollow tree where we kept house, me and Marcella and our friend Evadna Cheever; we didn't have no doll dishes, or just a few, so we used acorns, big ones, for our cups, and acorn caps for saucers. We made a little table out of a box, and hung a worn-out red tablecloth up at the door and, my, we wouldn't've changed it for a palace! . . . Nowdays I look at all them doll sets in the dime store: plastics and glassware and tin knives and forks, and I wonder if you young ones have half the fun we used to have pretending!"

"Maybe people always feel that way when they grow up," said Randy, who couldn't help wishing that reminiscence didn't bring out a tendency to lecture on the part of Cuffy.

"Maybe they do, I guess they do," agreed Cuffy. "I remember how my Grandma Lovell used to—but that's another story. Well, so we had our hollow tree, and our big hay loft, and our toboggan slides in winter, and black-ice on the slough to skate on. Oh, we had plenty to keep us busy, and happy, too. Mama was a wonderful cook, and Papa and Uncle Fisher and the hands and all us kids was wonderful eaters; if we ever left the table without feeling kind of bogged down and logy, we didn't think we'd been fed right. Pie all the time. Pie for breakfast always, and fried potatoes and pork. And all kinds of preserves and homemade bread and peach shortcake with yellow cream and hot, hot pans of biscuit and sweet butter——"

"It's a good thing John Doe can't talk human," Oliver said. "He'd be howling from hunger. Are there any cookies left?"

"I made some fresh this morning, help yourselves. You might give me one, too. . . . Well, so, I don't know just exactly how it happened, but what with Mama being the famous cook she was, and the farm so healthy and the milk so rich, the reputation spread, I guess, and one summer a family from Milwaukee came to board; a lady at least, and her two children; Mrs. Wellgrove, her name was, and her daughter, Ethel, was about Marcella's age and her son, Francis, was about mine. Ethel had been sick, she was mighty frail and peaked—guess that's why they come—and Francis he was a problem! In those days a lot of folks considered it stylish to dress their boys like Lord Fauntleroy—he was a boy in a storybook—and that meant they had to wear velvet pants and big lace collars and sometimes even a sash kind of dangling at the hip. Imagine! But the worst, awfullest feature about it was that they had to wear their hair long, too! Real long, down over their shoulders, like a girl, and, if possible, in curls besides. Course the curly-headed boys got the worst of it, and Francis, he was curly-headed; added to that his hair was red, so there he was, feeling like a boy and sure acting like one, but with all this mop, fiery red and hanging to his waist, and trimmed in fluffy bangs on his forehead into the bargain; well, you never saw anything like it. We never did. We'd heard about the Lord Fauntleroy book, of course, even out in the backwoods where we lived, but when we saw it come to life like that!—Homer, he was awful! He teased the poor boy so, and said even his name was a girl's, so of course Francis he had to act double bad and double loud and get himself double dirty just to show folks he was a boy all right in spite of all them curls and croshay collars and black silk sashes! We didn't understand that at the time; we just thought he was an awful nuisance. He tied the cows' tails together, and threw stones at the bull to get him riled up and put salt in the sugar bowl and vinegar in the sorghum and broke the shed windows and put a live turtle in Marcella's bed and ate half the marble cake that Mama had just baked for the Big Hollow Ladies' Aid Collation; that's only some of what he did, and we all got so we couldn't hardly stand the sight of him. Mrs. Wellgrove didn't seem to notice half of what went on; now and then she couldn't help but see, like the time he tied my best hat, my *only* good one, onto our big black ram and sent him galloping, and then she only said: "Fran—cis, Fran—cis. What will the little Meinhardts think of you?" Good thing she didn't know. "Someday I'm going to tie up his precious curls in the flypaper," Homer said, and I believe he would have, too, only for what happened later." Cuffy laughed heartily at her own memories.

"What *did* happen later?" insisted Oliver.

"Goodness, goodness, it don't seem so long ago," sighed Cuffy, still smiling. "What happened was this. There was lots of little islands in the Sac River; quantities of 'em in fact, but in the place where there was most of 'em the current was tricky; rapid and full of little whirlpools and eddies, and it was real deep, too. Papa and Mama never would let us swim or even wade in that part of the river. We knew that lots of people and even, once, a cow, had gotten caught in that current and drowned. So we left the place alone; and anyway we was allowed to play and swim all we wanted in the part of the river nearest the farm; it was safe there, and shallow and the water moved slow; some days, terrible hot days in July or August, we stayed in all afternoon long, and there wasn't a one of us couldn't swim.

"So one day long about the middle of August I found myself with no one else to play with but this pesky Francis Wellgrove; it was a tossup in my mind which would be worst, him or nobody. But I was a sociable girl, and I decided I'd try to stand him for a playmate just this once. Marcella and Homer had drove up to Indian Rocks with Papa to sell a load of melons. Mrs. Wellgrove and Ethel had gone to Madison to see the doctor, and Mama was in the house with Aunt Nettie, putting up preserves. Corn? Tomatoes? Don't remember. Albert Edward was too young to play with, and Evadna Cheever had the whooping cough. It was real lonesome. 'Let's us go swimming,' I says to Francis. It was awful hot. So we put on our suits (mine was an old blue dress) and went down to the river. Francis could swim, though not so good as we could, and it was all right when he wasn't ducking me or throwing mud. By and by we came out and went walking along the bank looking for cardinal flowers and lobelia—one's so red and one's so blue!—and we found a lot and picked a lot, and walked along the river bank talking and quarreling and slapping at gnats and pretty soon we came to the

islands and we went on walking. . . . But on one of
these islands there was a little house, or shed, all fallen
in and broken—been there years, I guess—and Francis
he saw it and said, 'What's that house for? Who built
it? What's in it?' 'I don't know,' I says. 'I never was to it;
none of us was.' And then I told him why, and about the
dangerous current and all and how we never went in
the water at that part of the Sac even to wade. So then he
wanted to get ahold of a boat, but there wasn't no boat
anywhere I knew of, and he kept on fussing and fussing
about that house and saying there might be something
valuable in it, money or old bones or a gun or something; and he wanted me to swim across with him and
explore it. Course I wouldn't, and I told him he couldn't,
but I could see he was getting his dander up, and first
thing I knew, all of a sudden, he threw down his bokay
of flowers and jumped in the river and started to swim!
Right away it was over his head and the current started
rushing him downstream fast as an express train, and
I ran along the bank still holding onto *my* bokay and
yelling at him to come back. He couldn't, though, and
halfway across he got panicky and screamed for me to
help him, with his face white and all his long hair stream-
ing out like a mermaid's; he began to gulp and breathe
water and I knew I'd have to go after him if he wasn't
to drown but, oh, heavenly day! Was I ever scared! So I
ran down the bank to below where he was, and then
I jumped in, praying out loud, and tried to swim across.
That water! It seemed to be alive, like a big strong snake,

it pulled so! But luckily I got ahold of Francis, grabbed him by his long hair, in fact, as he went past, and then when he tried to clutch and hang onto me, I slapped him hard as I could in the face and told him to lay still, there was no use trying to beat the current across or back. Don't know how I had the sense, but I figured if we just kept quiet and let it take us, we'd wind up somewheres. Did, too. One of these little islands had a dead tree leaning out from it. We fetched up on that, so hard it knocked the breath clean out of us, and then we had to take it sideways, hand over hand, with our legs half washing away from us, till we reached the island itself. Francis just laid down and was sick. I cried some, but in a couple of minutes we was both all right again, and then it seemed good—so good—just to lay there and breathe the warm air and feel the solid earth under us! Even the gnats seemed good. After a while Francis said, 'How we gointa get back?' I couldn't tell him. 'They'll find us,' I says, but I wasn't sure of it: not many folks came that way, no road or houses or anything, and as it turned out we never saw a mortal soul all that afternoon or evening; nothing but three strayed cows across the water, chewing and staring at us, and wandering away. The island we were on was small, bout 's big as this house I'd say, and there was nothing on it but spearmint and nettles and willow shoots. Nothing to eat. And then as evening came on the mosquitoes started up. My soul and body! They'd starved for generations, I guess, and we were like manna from heaven. I never was so bit, not all my life! They made me irritable so I snapped at Francis. 'It's all your own blame fault,' I says. 'You knew you wasn't supposed to go in that water! If you wasn't so stupid and so selfish and so proud of yourself we'd never been in this mess, neither one of us.' And he was humble about it. 'I know it,' he says. 'I don't know why I did it. I don't know why you'd ever forgive me. Saving my life and all, too.' Well, naturally that made me feel bad, so I said it was all right after all, and somebody'd be sure to find us. But the evening wore on and the mosquitoes kept biting and it was just pure misery, that's all, pure misery, and you know how it is: sharing a miserable predicament can make lifelong friends or enemies of a couple of folks. It made friends of us two. Between the slapping and the scratching we had to keep up all the while, we talked a lot. We confided in each other. One of the things Francis confided about was how he hated his long hair; he said his papa didn't like it either, but his mama's, Mrs. Wellgrove's, heart was set on it and there wasn't nothing they could do. 'I want to look like a boy,' he says, 'I want to look just like Homer.' So I had an idea and I said: 'If we ever get out of here and home I'll fix it so you'll get a haircut all right, and nobody'll be mad, either.' So anyway we were pretty good friends by the time night came, and that was lucky because it began to be real scary on that island; black as pitch, there wasn't a star overhead and not even a firefly that time of year. And then, well you wouldn't believe it, it began to rain! Yes, round about ten, eleven o'clock there was a thunderstorm, and out in Wisconsin those storms aren't the play-acting kind we have around here. I mean the sky splits open, wide open, and the ground shakes like fire engines was going over it, and the lightning licks around every place, not just one place, and it keeps a-going all the time; no stops between, where you can get your breath. The water, the rain, is solid, too; you might be sitting under a dam. Willow shoots, even willow trees, aren't much to shelter under; their leaves are always kind of stingy. We had no place to hide, so we just cuddled close together and bowed our heads and prayed the lightning wouldn't strike us. We never slept one wink. The storm kept up and up and then went off down river, and then came back and played with us all over again like some big mean cat with two wet mice! But finally it went away and the night was over. Oh, I never saw a morning as beautiful as that! The mist laid on the river in a band; you couldn't see the river, only hear it, and the sun was red and lighted every single drop on every leaf so it was red, too, like a ruby, and birds flew in and out of the mist, appearing and disappearing, and the air all smelt of mint and water. On a morning like that you couldn't help but hope, no matter if you was bone-soaked and hungry and a child."

"When did they find you, though?" demanded Oliver, breaking Cuffy's silence.

"Soon after that. Very soon. My father he'd been down there twice during the night, but his lantern had blew out, and we couldn't hear his shouting for the racket of the storm. In the morning we could, though, and he and Uncle Fisher got a rowboat and launched it well upstream and across on the diagonal and fetched us off the bank and we was safe!"

Randy took a deep sniff from the coffee canister which she had forgotten about during the story.

"What I can't see is why you never told us this before," said Oliver.

"Modesty, I bet, that's why," said Randy. "Because she saved that boy's life. Isn't that why, Cuffy?"

"Oh, I don't know. Just never thought of it I guess."

"Certainly not. It was modesty," said Randy, convinced. "Some people are that way; if it was me I'd boast. But you still haven't explained that pin."

"Or about the guy's curls," said Oliver. "Did you get them cut for him?"

"Course I did," said Cuffy. "Nothing to it. A day or two later I took him berrying with me; and it just so happened that I knew of a good burdock patch, and I collected a fine bunch of burrs and did a job of hairdressing on Francis, paying special attention to the bangs. 'Now, France,' I says (because that's what we'd took to calling him), 'don't you tell no lies, but just try not to say exactly *how* you got these burrs in your hair.' He handled it pretty good. 'Why, Mama,' he says, 'you never *saw* so many burrs, and I just got all messed up in 'em. I had to get down so low under a barbwire fence.' (That was true, too, only the fence wasn't right near the burrs.)

'I don't know what I'da done if it hadn't been for Evangeline.' (No one called me Cuffy then, naturally.) 'She's saved my life twice, she has.' Well, I admit that none of that was real lies, but it wasn't the honest truth, either, and it wasn't very honorable of us." Cuffy looked searchingly at her audience.

"Okay, Cuffy dear," said Randy. "We understand the moral. But what about the pin?"

"So naturally Francis had to have his hair cut short. I'd done a real thorough burr-matting job; his mama, Mrs. Wellgrove, had tears in her eyes all the time Papa was shearing him. 'My baby is gone,' she kept moaning. 'My little prince is gone forever.' I'm sure it was partly that word 'forever' that made Francis grin the way he did, pleased as Punch. And when the curls was laying on the floor around the chair and Papa finished up the job, there wasn't nothing of the prince about Francis: he was just a redheaded, snub-nosed boy, nine years old and no nonsense about it. . . . So then the pin. It was a pin of Mrs. Wellgrove's and she thought the world of it, always wore it; but the morning that Papa got us off that island and Francis told her how I'd saved his life (course he exaggerated it a lot) she unpinned it from her collar right then and there, took Mr. Wellgrove's photo out of it, and fastened it onto my dress. 'Think of us when you wear this,' she says, 'and how we're always grateful to you.' . . . She was a real emotional impulsive lady. Mr. Wellgrove, now, he was different. He come up to get his family in September, and he was a big, jolly man with a dark red face, a prosperous brewer. His mustache was yellow, I remember, and he brought presents to us all, wonderful presents: a music box for me, I know, with a bird on top, and a Made-in-Germany doll with gold hair and eyes that closed, and he took me aside and told me how he was real pleased that I'd saved his son's life and all, but just equally pleased about the fate of them curls (Francis must have told him), and Mrs. Wellgrove, she gave me the little photo of her son, and this, too. Look."

Cuffy pried up the tiny oval glass and then the child's picture beneath; under that, pressed against the gold, was a round ringlet like a coil of fine red copper wire.

"His? Francis Wellgrove's? After all these years?" It looked so young, so living still, as if it had been clipped an hour ago from some child's curly head.

"Yes, his," said Cuffy. "My sister Marcella, she saw him in Milwaukee ten, eleven years ago and—wouldn't you know it?—he was bald as a doorknob, she told me. Rich and bald, but he'd turned out to be a real nice man, she said."

"What happened to his sister Ethel, did she get better?" Randy wanted to know.

"Oh, Ethel! Why she grew up and went to Europe and married a real live prince. Eyetalian. I always knew how much that must please her mama who had a high opinion of princes from the way she talked. . . . Oh, we heard from 'em for years, the whole family, and

Francis always sent me birthday presents. He was a nice little boy after his hair got cut and even before it, I realize now. Yes, they were lovely people and that was a lovely, lovely summer."

Cuffy sighed and yawned. She snapped the brooch shut and put it back, haphazard, where it belonged.

"All right, now," she said, getting to her feet. "It's late! Good gracious, look how late it is! I'm going to start supper right away, and I need space. Whatever you're looking for don't look for it in *here*. In half an hour, Randy, you can set the table. And someone please let the dogs out."

Randy and Oliver let themselves out, too, watching the dogs hurtling around the lawn, ears flying.

"It's funny how you can know a person all your life," said Oliver, "and still there's secrets to find out."

"It's half nice and half horrid," agreed Randy. "But I suppose it keeps things interesting. Doesn't it?" she asked a little doubtfully.

"Hmm. I wonder if *Willy's* got any secrets we don't know about," said Oliver in another tone entirely, and they went off to find him.

Willy Sloper had his own apartment over the stable. Long ago, in New York, he had been the Melendys' furnace man. When they had moved to the country, naturally, they had asked him to come along, for the whole family loved him, and he could do anything: plumbing, carpentry, house-painting, and even—as he had proved since they had lived here—farming, landscaping, animal husbandry and gardening. He also knew how to cook, whittle, and play the recorder.

They found him in the stable, grooming Lorna Doone, the brown horse. Jess and Damon, the team of work horses had been loaned out indefinitely to Mr. Addison, a farmer friend.

"What'll we do?" whispered Randy. "We can't just go and start searching him, very well."

"I'll fix it," said Oliver and went right up to Willy and asked him, politely, of course, to show them everything that was in his pockets.

"We have a reason for this, Willy," Randy assured him anxiously. "It's not just, you know, frivolity."

"Cops after me again?" asked Willy good-naturedly, and emptied out his pockets and showed them what he had: a dollar bill and thirty-seven cents; a pair of pliers, a monkey wrench, three pencils, a handkerchief, a cough drop, a small can of machine oil, a comb with five teeth missing, a pack of cards and a watch. No clue.

"May I please examine the inside of your cap, Willy?" asked Oliver; but that revealed nothing either.

"Have you noticed any writing about your person lately?" inquired Randy. The question sounded very peculiar even as she asked it, and she did not wonder that Willy burst out laughing.

"No, not just lately," he said. "The only writing about my person that I know of is that tattoo-piece I got on my left arm, and that's been there for thirty years, and all it says is Mabel."

"No, we know about that one, of course," said Oliver. "Well, thanks just the same, Willy. Sorry to trouble you."

He and Randy returned to the house, perplexed and curious.

About two weeks later when all hope of finding the clue had been abandoned, or at least suspended, Randy decided to give Isaac a bath; the flea situation had reached its usual autumnal pitch, and she had bought a bar of soap that smelled as if it would kill anything. She ran water into the laundry tub, put on her raincoat and rolled up the sleeves, located Isaac cowering under the bottom shelf of the linen closet (he always seemed able to distinguish the sound of water being run for his bath from the sound of water being run for any other purpose) and carried him trembling and faintly growling down to the kitchen. She unfastened his collar and laid it on the drainboard (Cuffy was not there to stop her) and deposited Isaac in the warm water. All the time that she was scrubbing and he was groaning, she was aware of an idea in her mind that she was too busy to examine. She scrubbed and soaped and rinsed, and in his saturated state Isaac was revealed as a much smaller, less important-looking dog than when he was dry and fluffy. (Perhaps that was one of the reasons for his horror of baths.) The air positively pulsed with the odor of strong disinfectant as whole flea communities gave up the ghost and a large lake of spilled water widened on the floor. After the final rinsing Randy lifted her shuddering victim from the tub, wrapped him warmly in an old towel, and murmured words of praise and consolation. Holding him in her lap she started to dry him, and as she did so the idea which had lurked behind her thoughts sprang forward vividly. *Isaac's collar!* There it lay on the drainboard, a loop of worn red leather with its small brass license plate and the dangling metal capsule that contained his name and address. Randy sprang to her feet, the towel fell to the floor and Isaac, released, flew from the kitchen, scattering showers, to dry himself in his own way, on the living-room rug. Randy's fingers trembled as she unscrewed the capsule. Within it, as she had suddenly foreseen, was a tiny roll of blue paper.

"Oliver! Oliver!" she shouted, nobly refusing to read what was written on it until her brother could read it too.

"What do you want?" shouted Oliver from the Office, two flights up. "I'm busy, I'm trying to make gold with my chemical set."

Since Cuffy was not at home Randy could shout the news at the top of her lungs.

"The clue! The clue! I found it. Hurry!"

Oliver got down the first flight of stairs partly by falling, and down the second by way of the bannister. and was at her side almost before she had stopped shouting.

"The collar!" he exclaimed. " 'Call me and I will

come' . . . Holy cow. We should have thought of Isaac first thing! Read it out, Randy, I can't read script very good."

Randy read the clue aloud:

"Named for a jewel, named for a bird,
Asleep for threescore years and ten,
First find my resting place, and then,
Stepping toward sunrise, find the third
Strange clue that marks the secret way
To rare reward and a fair summer day."

CHAPTER III

The Resting Place

Named for a jewel, named for a bird,
 Asleep for threescore years and ten,
 First find my resting place, and then,
Stepping toward sunrise, find the third
 Strange clue that marks the secret way
 To rare reward and a fair summer day.

"A SUMMER DAY!" exclaimed Oliver. "Gosh! Does that
mean we're never going to get to the end of this
thing till *summer?* Why it's only just begun to be October now!"

"I know," said Randy slowly. "But I wonder—I
think it's been invented, this game or search or whatever

44

it is, by somebody who understands the way we feel with all the others gone; someone who wants to give us something pleasant to think about instead of just groaning around the house and missing them all the time. I'm glad it's going to last a long time."

"I guess I am too, kind of. But what can it be, do you think? And who could have thought it up? I don't think Cuffy could write poetry like that, and I'm pretty sure Willy couldn't either."

"If it wasn't for the way the things are said, I'd believe it was Rush," said Randy. "Or it *could* be Father. But he's been away so long this time I don't see how he could have planted the clues. Mona might have written the poems, I suppose, but it's not her handwriting and it doesn't look faked; it looks sort of easy and dashed-off, as if it was written in a hurry by someone who'd written that way for years and years; someone very grown-up."

"Yes, but what about this clue, now," said Oliver, anxious to take up the scent again. " 'Named for a jewel, named for a bird.' What could *that* mean, for cat's sake?"

"Threescore years and ten, too. That's seventy years. *Asleep* for that long, it must mean somebody dead."

"I've heard that toads can sleep an awful long time," offered Oliver hopefully.

"No, it's somebody dead, I'm sure, and that means a cemetery, I should think. That must be it; a gravestone somewhere, and a certain name."

"There's a graveyard in Carthage, and another one —a big one—in Braxton, and there's others around, too. I s'pose we'll have to search them all. But what could the name be? Jewel and bird. I don't get it."

"Well, it could be a name like Pearl-uh-Stork, for instance," said Randy, without much conviction. "Or Opal Owl. Something like that."

Opal Owl struck Oliver as immensely funny; so funny, in fact, that he found it necessary to lie down on the kitchen linoleum and thrash with his heels in an excess of mirth. "Opal Ow-owl!" he yelled. "Opal Owl! Oh, gosh, oh, gee, what about Diamond Turkey, for instance? What about Emerald Eagle?"

"You're being terribly silly," said Randy with quiet dignity. "Sometimes I forget how young you still are. Now look, you're all wet, you've rolled right into a puddle of Isaac's bath water, and you're going to smell terribly of flea soap."

Oliver arose, somewhat sobered, and Randy got the mop and removed the puddle. But there was nothing she could do about the living-room carpet which bore large damp traces of Isaac's attempts to dry himself. Isaac himself was discovered, somewhat disheveled, under the desk in Father's study. After Randy had hauled him out, she took him to the back porch to brush and comb him. All the time her mind was busy with thoughts of the clue: locations, and the names of birds and jewels. Evidently Oliver was similarly occupied, for now and then he called down to her from the Office window.

"There's a family named Gull in Carthage," he shouted. "Gloria Gull is in my class. Maybe she had an ancestor with a jewel name."

"Ask her tomorrow," shouted Randy in reply. "Or no, don't. Suppose she didn't? She'd think you were crazy. We'd better just look in the graveyard."

Silence. Then Oliver's voice.

"Should we go look now?"

"Oh, it'll be dark too soon, and I have stacks of homework. We'll look tomorrow."

Another silence; then another shout.

"Herron! Mark's our brother, now, and called Melendy; but his name *was* Herron before we adopted him and that's a bird's name, too."

"Spelled differently, but I don't suppose it matters," yelled Randy. "Only his family didn't come from around here."

Cuffy arrived at that moment. She had walked home from the village where she had gone to have a cup of tea with Mrs. Ed Wheelwright and obtain a recipe for jelly doughnuts.

"My lands, what's all this hollering about?" was her first remark. "I could hear you clear up on the highway, bellowing like cattle on a prairie. Lost cattle bellowing."

"Could you hear what we were saying?" asked Randy.

"No, just the tone of voice."

"That's good, though it wasn't anything wrong.

We just shouted because Oliver was busy in the Office
and I was busy down here and we had things to tell
each other. Look, isn't Isaac beautiful?"

"Yes, he is," said Cuffy warmly. "You've done a
real good job." She took off her shoes and sighed. "Oh,
my feet. That's a long walk when you're stout like I
am. I'll be glad to get to heaven and be given wings."

"Don't you talk that way!" scolded Randy. "You
have to live just as long as we do, Cuffy, and help take
care of all our children. You rest there, now, and I'll go
up and get your slippers."

Cuffy sat where she was, smiling contentedly.
They're turning out real nice, she thought; they're
lovely children, all of 'em. I never really worried.

Nevertheless she was rather puzzled when Oliver
and Randy for the next two days spent the hours after
school in the Carthage cemetery, arriving home a little
late for supper; and she was something more than
puzzled on Saturday when they requested a picnic lunch
and announced that they were going to Braxton "to
spend the day in the graveyard."

"I can't understand why you're all of a sudden so
taken up with tombstones," grumbled Cuffy. "I declare
I wonder if it's healthy."

"It's research we're doing, Cuff," said Randy. "The
inscriptions on old tombstones are very interesting;
some of the Carthage ones go back to seventeen thirty.
When people have been dead as long as they have, you
don't think of them as real at all; more like people in a

book, invented people. Some of them had pretty names."

"Some of them had funny ones," said Oliver. "Gideon Wallop, for instance. Gottlieb Fusswinkel."

"Oh, you're making them up," scoffed Cuffy.

"No, honest I'm not! I can show them to you, both of them, in Carthage cemetery. Simeon Snail, too."

"But there are pretty ones as well," insisted Randy. "Araminta Carew, for instance: she died when she was seventeen, in eighteen hundred and six. And Sophronisba Stellway. *She* lived to be a hundred."

"Some of the poems on them, though, gee!" said Oliver. " 'Smile not, oh, passer-by, beware! The next opening sepulchre may yawn for thee,' " he quoted, shivering comfortably.

The truth was that the young Melendys were acquiring a taste for old cemeteries. There was something very peaceful, they thought, about the quiet places; the tilted stones patched with lichens, standing in a bee-humming tangle of myrtle and wild asters. It was pleasant to walk between the stones, tracing the half-eroded names, the epitaphs, some beautiful, some sadly funny, some grotesque. Pleasant as it was, however, they had not, so far, found the clue they sought. Plenty of jewel names, yes: Pearls and Rubys and Opals galore. Plenty of bird names, too; Finch and Wren and Crane and Quayle and even Raven. But not one combination of jewel and bird together.

The Braxton cemetery also failed to solve the riddle, and it was not nearly such a pleasant place to wander, being far too grand and modern and well-groomed. The monuments were glossy and severe, the grass more like a stiff plush rug than grass, and the flowers were planted in such uncompromising designs that they did not seem live flowers at all, but imitations made of crepe paper and buckram. The children found themselves whispering, and tiptoeing along the perfect paths.

"It's like a field full of big stone furniture," said Oliver. "It hasn't anything to do with people."

"And the trees, too," Randy said. "All they've got is weeping willows and those purple beech trees, such mournful, serious trees. *I* wouldn't like it here."

It was a large place, and they were conscientious in their search; in the end they came away depressed and tired.

"I'm almost ready to give up," said Randy. "I don't ever want to see another grave."

"Me, either," sighed Oliver. "I don't think I ever want to be buried even."

"My mind's all seething with names and dates. When I close my eyes tonight I know I'll see nothing but letters carved on tombstones. Honestly, it's—it's gloomy."

They rode along in silence, slowly. The wind was against them all the way.

"Randy!" cried Oliver suddenly. "I bet I know where it is! Why didn't we think of it sooner! They didn't mean for it to be so hard——"

"But where? Tell me!" demanded Randy.

"Why, you know, that little old, old graveyard up near the hill on the place where Mark used to live? The one where there used to be a church that got struck by lightning?"

"That's where Mona and I got lilies of the valley last spring; they grow wild there. I bet that's it!" cried Randy. "Oliver, you're a genius. Only we'll have to wait till tomorrow. It's late, and anyway I couldn't face another today."

"Well, the clue *said* step toward the sunrise, or something like that, remember. We'll get up early and go on our bikes."

It seemed a fine idea at the time; less splendid in the somber dark of five o'clock next morning. Randy had slept with the kitchen alarm clock under her pillow so that it would be muffled when it rang, and stifled quickly. Its hearty tick came pounding right through the pillow into her ear, but it did not keep her awake as long as she had supposed that it would; not more than seven minutes at the most. Its morning peal was something else, however, and brought her out of sleep with a shout of panic; she quickly shut it off and went to rouse Oliver as stealthily as overwhelming drowsiness permitted. It took some time for Oliver to begin co-operating. All he would say was the word "no," spoken firmly, and he kept rolling himself up in his blankets again as often as she unrolled him.

"Then I'm going alone," said Randy at last, in desperation.

That brought him out of bed; grumbling and stumbling and reluctant, but on his way nonetheless, and soon they were out of doors in the chill dim morning, riding bicycles still wet with hoarfrost, down the shadowed road.

"Morning's never any good till after breakfast," said Oliver.

"My teeth are chattering; are yours?" said Randy. "Why did they decide on sunrise, do you suppose? Why not sunset?"

Oliver did not answer. They rode without speaking. Every farmhouse they passed was silent, but from the barns there issued a tinkle and a clank, and the roosters everywhere were crowing.

"I don't see how they always know what time it is," said Oliver. "I don't see why they *care* so much."

A band of palest light lay in the east; the morning star, fresh as a raindrop, sparkled in the sky, and the first breeze of the day moved in the trees and shook the papery tatters of the corn shocks. The world was brushed with a spiderweb of frost.

Tipped on a hillside, closed in its low crumbled wall, lay the forgotten churchyard. It was half overgrown; some of the headstones had fallen flat and been lashed to the earth with brambles and bindweed; others slanted sideways or leaned together, their tops just clear of the gone-to-seed goldenrod tassels and pods of Queen Anne's lace curled up like nests for hummingbirds. An apple tree had taken root there, long ago. It leaned above the wall and dropped its leaves and apples on the earth.

In the growing light Oliver and Randy were at work; parting the vines and brambles, reading the forgotten, ancient names.

"Henrietta Ponsonby, Nathaniel Ponsonby. Lucretia Vane, Jared Vane, Octavius Elisha Vane. Darius Todworthy . . . Poor Darius, he's all alone, there's not another Todworthy in sight."

The east was brightening, was topaz-colored, and a little school of clouds swam in the sky above it, bright as goldfishes.

"The time is going, we must hurry," whispered Randy. The hour, the place, both caused her to whisper, and when Oliver came upon the stone that stood alone beneath the apple tree, it was in a whisper that he called his sister.

"Here it is. I've found it."

Randy came and stood beside him.

"Garnet Swann," she read aloud. "Beloved wife of Jared Swann. Yes, Oliver, you've found the place at last, and look, she's been asleep three quarters of a century."

Now the sun edged upward, red as a rose, benevolent, allowing mortal eyes to view it. Later it would blind them. The valley was bathed in a pink light, the hills were clear and dark. Frost turned to dew and sparkled on the grass.

"We must walk toward it. Now," said Randy.

With ritual steps they marched slowly through the wet tall weeds and briars, looking up and down. They came to the wall; they found nothing.

"If we just knew what to look for," said Oliver in a worried voice. "Do you think it means for us to go over the wall? We don't know how *far* east."

"I don't think so, let's go back and start again," said Randy, so they went back to the stone marked Garnet Swann and walked again toward the sunrise. This time, when they came to the wall, they examined it carefully. It was very old, and grey-green lichens were stuck flat against the stones. One lichen, larger than the rest and growing just inside the wall, under a jutting stone, looked rather strange. No wonder, either, since closer inspection showed that it was held in place, most unnaturally, by strips of Scotch tape.

"Aha!" said Randy quietly, detaching it.

"What will they think of next!" exclaimed Oliver, sounding so exactly like Cuffy that Randy burst out laughing.

Underneath it, of course, was the folded clue; somewhat lichen-stained and dented by irregularities in the stone against which it had been pressed—how long?— but still quite legible.

"It's in poetry again, of course," said Randy. "This is what it says:

"Well done! Now leave the sleeping acre to its peace.
   The sun is risen; let it light the road.

Named for an emperor, in my abode,
The fourth imprisoned clue awaits release:
   Beneath, the hours tell their names and go.
   Above, a voice was silenced long ago."

"They get tougher," said Oliver at last. "I don't know *what* they're talking about now."

"We'll work it out though," said Randy, success having gone to her head. "I'm not going to be a dancer when I grow up, or an artist either. I'm going to be a counterespionage agent. You can be one, too; Melendy and Melendy, Counterspies. We'll have it on the door like that. We'll have to wear disguises all the time: beards for you and all kinds of queer-shaped mustaches, and I will dye my hair a different color every week and learn to speak with an accent."

Oliver did not think highly of this flight of fancy. He ignored it.

"Brother, I'm hungry," he said. "Hunting clues makes you awful hungry."

They pushed through the wet tangle, soaked to the knees, to where their bicycles lay beside the road. The melted hoarfrost flashed from every blade and stem; the old tree dropped an apple and a handful of leaves.

"I wouldn't mind being buried here," said Randy. "Right out in the country with cows and birds around and lots of space."

"Better than that big stone furniture store in Braxton," Oliver agreed. "It's kind of nice here, kind of cozy."

Their bikes flew like the wind, down the hills, around the curves. From every house came hot, sharp smells of bacon and coffee and toast. Randy and Oliver, hungry as wolves and happy as larks, sang at the tops of their lungs all the way home.

Their house smelled of breakfast, too. It was a welcome sight, always: square, broad, comfortable, with its mansard roof and little cupola set like a cap on the very top. They loved that house, all of them. It still lay in the early-morning shadow of the hill behind it. The spruce trees were grave ornaments, and the iron deer on the front lawn seemed animals transfixed; all was silent and motionless. But in the next second the kitchen door burst open and the dogs, Isaac and John Doe, shot out, wild with the delight of morning; barking and whirling and skidding and stopping short to sniff. When they saw Oliver and Randy they came careening toward them with their ears flying and their eyes rolling. "Why didn't you take us with you?" they demanded, in barks, and Cuffy in the doorway said, "My lands! Where *was* you? I was just going up to wake you!"

"Well, we took a spin to the old graveyard back of the Meeker place," said Oliver.

"Not *again?*" This time Cuffy looked really concerned. "Not *another* cemetery."

Randy let her bike fall with a crash to the ground;

she went up to Cuffy and gave her a good big squeeze around the middle.

"It's the last one, Cuffy darling. No more cemeteries for us. Could I have two fried eggs this morning?"

"Could I have three?" said Oliver.

CHAPTER IV

The Emperor's Abode

Well done! Now leave the sleeping acre to its peace.
   The sun is risen; let it light the road.
   Named for an emperor, in my abode,
The fourth imprisoned clue awaits release:
   Beneath, the hours tell their names and go.
   Above, a voice was silenced long ago.

"WHO DO we know that's got an emperor's name?" said Oliver. "I can't *remember* any emperors."

"There isn't anyone I know of that's named Nero," said Randy. "Nero's the only one I can think of at the moment. No, wait, Napoleon was an emperor."

"Well, who do you know that's named *Napoleon,* for Pete's sake?" inquired Oliver rather sensibly.

They were on their way home from school, riding their bicycles through the golden October haze.

"And there were hundreds of emperors," said Randy thoughtfully. "Goodness, there were emperors in Rome and China and Austria and France even—why, when you think of it, the emperors in history are a dime a dozen."

"Aren't there any left?" Oliver seemed a little sad. An emperor sounded like a splendid being: proud, dazzling, more than mortal, with rays of light around him like the petals of a sunflower.

"No, no more. A few kings, only, and some queens. Nowadays most countries are run by a man, or a lot of men, in business suits. In a few countries the most important man does wear a uniform, but still he isn't called a king, though he's treated like one. He's called Marshal or Generalissimo or something like that, and his uniforms are severe and unjoyful looking."

"Gee, too bad," said Oliver.

"If only Father was home," said Randy. "He knows everything about history; he'd give us all the names we needed. Who do we know, think, Oliver, that has an emperorish name?"

"What about Frederick?" asked Oliver tentatively. "Wasn't there an emperor named Frederick, somewhere or other, haven't I heard? How about Mr. Frederick, the butcher?"

"Oliver!" cried Randy, in delight, falling off her bicycle—though not seriously. "Of course there was! I'm sure you've done it again! Let's go right back now, and see."

"No, wait a minute," said Oliver, who was less impulsive than Randy and liked to have things, as far as possible, planned in advance. "We'd better be sure where to look for the clue when we get to Mr. Frederick's. What does it mean: 'Beneath, the hours tell their names and go'?"

"Oh, I have that one figured out. It must be a clock, or a sundial; maybe it could be a watch, even!"

"It could be a radio," Oliver suggested. "*They're* always telling what the hour is."

"Maybe. But what about that silent voice above?"

"Well. . . . It could be a radio on a table with a picture of George Washington over it, or some other dead famous person that talked a lot and made speeches. I mean it *could be*," said Oliver, his imagination running riot.

"It might be the clock on the Carthage courthouse tower; the bell in the top hasn't been rung since the war ended."

"Brother, I'd like it to be there!" said Oliver, who saw himself hanging from the tower with Randy leaning out of the belfry and holding him by the heels. He could imagine the little blue paper, wedged in a crack in the wall, and the pale, upturned faces in the street below.

"It would be hard to keep it a secret if they hid it there, though," said Randy, in whose mind a somewhat similar scene had been enacted. In this case, though, it was she who had hung head down to grasp the prize. "And anyway, name me an emperor who inhabits the Carthage courthouse!"

The next day, after school, they stopped in at Mr. Klaus Frederick's meat store. Randy had prudently asked Cuffy to let her do the marketing for once. As she had never asked to do this in her life before, Cuffy had thought it wise to encourage her.

"Why, I guess so, child. Here, I'll make a list. The family's smaller now, so I'm sure you and Oliver can fit the parcels into your bicycle baskets."

Mr. Frederick's meat store was a clean, blank place with sawdust on the floor. They had never been in it before, only seen it as they passed by. Cuffy patronized another, Gus Vogeltree's, farther down the street. This was a less jolly place. Beyond the shop there was another room, darker, where they could see big beef carcasses hanging from meathooks, ghostly in the gloom.

Mr. Frederick looked like a piece of meat himself— a cut of beef—red in the face, jowly, with two large hands, like steaks, placed on the counter before him. He wore a tight white apron, rather soiled, a stiff straw hat, and a pencil behind his ear. He did not smile.

"Well, kids, what'll it be?"

Randy read from her list: "Six pork chops, please. And two pounds of round steak, ground. And have you any beef heart for our dogs?"

"I got beef heart, I don't know if it's for your dogs," said Mr. Frederick ungenially.

While Randy was ordering, Oliver's eyes were darting about the shop; at the big pale carcasses on the meathooks, the picked chickens lined up like little arks under the counter glass, the calendar high on the wall —and then, yes, his heart stopped, or almost did—for just below the calendar was an old-fashioned wall clock in a hexagonal wooden case, with a brass pendulum stepping sedately below it. The picture on the calendar above it was the thing! For, believe it or not, it was a picture of George Washington! Oliver felt that this was definitely an omen, and he was certain that on top of the clockcase a clue was waiting to be found. He kicked Randy, who said "Ow," and when Mr. Frederick had turned aside to grind the round steak he pointed to the calendar.

"George Washington, like I said," he whispered.

"I know, I noticed," Randy murmured, looking at him in awe. "Oliver, I wonder if you've got second sight? Because you could be rich and famous if——"

But Oliver was not interested in such speculations.

"How'll we get it?" he demanded in a whisper. Mr. Frederick, they both knew, would probably not be co-operative about letting them examine the clock. He would want to know why. He might be indignant. Nevertheless, Oliver decided to try to win him to friendliness.

"This certainly is a nice store," he said enthusiastically. "It certainly is nice and clean and everything."

Mr. Frederick did not reply. He slapped the ground meat onto a sheet of brown paper and twiddled some string off of a big spool on the counter.

"Is this your abode?" inquired Oliver.

This time Mr. Frederick looked up, possibly startled. "My what?" he said.

"Your ab—your house. Where you live."

Mr. Frederick counted out six pork chops, slapped them onto another piece of brown paper, twiddled more string off the spool, and tied up the parcel. He took the pencil from behind his ear and holding it between his blunt red fingers—like frankfurters—he looked at Oliver.

"You kidding?" he said.

"Why, no," said Oliver hastily. "Gee, no, I just——"

"And the beef heart, please," said Randy firmly, interrupting. "For our dogs."

Oliver stared at the clock in anguish. His attempt to placate Mr. Frederick had failed conspicuously. How would they ever, now, be able to reach the clue?

Mr. Frederick slapped the beef heart onto still another piece of paper, tied it up, and once again took the pencil from behind his ear.

"That'll be three fifty," he said. "Hope you kids got it. We don't give no credit here."

"Here's a five-dollar bill," said Randy haughtily. "I hope *you* have *change*."

She felt discouraged; so did Oliver. Nothing had been accomplished, and Cuffy would be cross at the price they'd paid for the meat.

At that moment a telephone rang in the room behind the shop. Mr. Frederick went to answer it. Halfway there he turned and came back, carefully picking up the five-dollar bill from the counter where Randy had laid it and taking it with him. He's afraid we'd run off with it and the meat too, thought Randy, shocked.

"Now!" said Oliver as they heard Mr. Frederick say "hello" into the phone.

The clock was high on the wall; there was no chair or stool behind the counter. As though they had rehearsed it, Randy lifted Oliver as high as she could (he was heavy, rather a fat little boy, and she couldn't help grunting with effort), and Oliver deftly ran his hand along the top of the clockcase. He felt a deposit of dust and grit, touched something hard and small, and clenched it in his fist just as Mr. Frederick came back into the shop.

For a second no one moved. They stood as they were, ridiculously; Oliver still lifted from the floor in

Randy's aching arms; Mr. Frederick transfixed in the doorway. His red face grew purple, eggplant color; his little eyes were the palest blue, almost white; it was astonishing how fierce they looked.

"What do you kids think you're doin'?"

His loud voice, wavering with rage, released the spell. Randy dropped Oliver with a thud and automatically flexed her tired arms. "We—why, we were just looking for something," she said lamely.

"Lookin' for something! In my store? Lookin' for what? You tell me the truth, see, or I'll get the cops after you. Gointa get 'em anyhow!"

"We weren't doing anything wrong, really we weren't!" Randy tried to explain. "People, friends of ours, have been hiding things for us to find; sort of like a treasure hunt, you know. We thought—they led us to believe—they'd hidden one of them here. On your clock we thought, maybe."

"You have got the same name as an emperor, you know," said Oliver helpfully.

"What do you think I am? Dumb? Green? Born yesterday?" inquired Mr. Frederick. "N-a-a, you don't. Stay right there where you are a minute." His left hand, still holding the five-dollar bill, lightly touched the handle of a butcher knife lying on the counter, his other reached out and opened up the cash register; after a hasty appraisal of its contents, he clanged it shut again, reached around the doorjamb behind him, still glaring at the young Melendys, and pulled out a chair.

"Stay where you are, see," he ordered (unnecessarily, as it happened, for the children stood frozen where they were). They watched, like terrified rabbits, as Mr. Frederick bounded up on the chair and lifted the calendar from its hook above the clock. They saw, now, why it was hung so high, for it was used to conceal the little wall safe which Mr. Frederick was now engaged in opening. They watched him as he peered and counted, satisfying himself that nothing was missing.

"All right," he said, slamming the heavy little door and replacing the calendar. He stepped down remarkably lightly from his stool, and faced them like a pirate still grasping the long sharp knife and the five-dollar bill. For some reason the things he wore—the long tight apron, like a skirt, the hard black-banded hat, the jaunty pencil tilted beside a face so far from jaunty—made him doubly terrifying.

"All right," he said, advancing on them slowly. "But now get out, see? Get out and don't come meddling again. And if you ever mention to anyone—to a single person, see?—about how you saw my safe or where it is, I'll find it out, see? And I'll skin you both alive!" With this he brandished the knife, and Randy made for the door. It was Oliver who remembered to snatch up the parcels from the counter; then he, too, was in the street beside her.

"What a horrible—what a *terrible* man!" gasped Randy.

"He never gave us our change, either," said Oliver.

"Wild horses couldn't drag me back to get it," cried Randy. "But what will Cuffy say? How could they have sent us to that awful place? And all for nothing, too."

"Hey, wait," said Oliver, stopping in the street. "It may not be for nothing; I think I've got the clue." He reached into his pocket and drew out the little object he had snatched from the top of the clock frame.

He and Randy stared at it, lying on his palm.

"The clock key," said Randy quietly. In a minute they began to laugh. They laughed so hard that they had to go over and lean against the wall of the Carthage Municipal and Farmer's Loan and Trust Building until they recovered. People went by them on their way home —it was five o'clock—and smiled in sympathy, wishing they knew the joke.

"Fair exchange is no robbery," Randy said. "We have the key, but he's got a dollar and a half of ours."

"I think," she said a little later, as they were riding home, "that I have just about a dollar and a half left in my bank. Maybe I'd just better give it to Cuffy as the change; you know, without saying anything."

"Yes, and then she won't have to ask questions and be worried," said Oliver piously. "I'll chip in fifteen cents; it's all I've got."

When they coasted down the driveway to their house, the Four-Story Mistake, they could see the lighted windows shining. Randy sighed.

"It costs a lot to do the marketing," she said.

The next day she and Oliver took great satisfaction

in composing and sending a letter to Mr. Frederick. It said:

Dear Sir,
    "A dollar and a half seems exsorbitent for a clock key, does it not? But accept it please, and you may keep the change.

                                        Yours sincerely,
                                        The Robbers

A few days later Randy had a new idea about the clue. It came to her in the middle of her English History class at ten thirty in the morning, and struck her with such force that when Miss Kipkin asked her to name the originator of the Magna Carta she answered "Beethoven."

She advanced her theory to Oliver that afternoon on their way home.

"I'm going straight up to the Office when we get back and look at the Victrola records," she told him. "Beethoven *did* compose a piano concerto called the 'Emperor,' you know. I've got it all figured out. The Emperor concerto book should be on one of the shelves, and the next record under it could be 'The Dance of the Hours'—I'm sure we've still got it—and the next one *over* it could be one of the Caruso records—he died long ago and was the best singer in the world—or maybe one of Richard Tauber's. We've *got* all those, and I bet we'll find the clue among them, and if we do we'll *know* it's

Rush who thought it up; he's always been the boss of the records!"

As she said this she thought of her eldest brother, industriously printing the names of musical compositions in ink on little strips of adhesive tape and sticking them onto the backs of the record albums. He had not cut the strips long enough and could not keep his printing small enough, so that on these labels Tchaikovsky was irreverently tagged as Tchai, and Beethoven appeared as Beet. Chopin, of course, was Chop, and Debussy became Deb. The compositions and performers were similarly abbreviated with the result that every symphony was a symp. and every orchestra an orc.

Oliver was deeply impressed with Randy's idea, and as soon as they got home they slammed their books down on the kitchen table and pounded up the two flights of stairs to the Office. This was a beloved room, the children's own, cluttered with all the evidence and litter of their hobbies, interests, tastes, talents, and works in progress. Rush's careworn upright piano stood against one wall, Mona's masks and costumes hung on a row of pegs. Oliver's electric train and tracks sprawled across the floor; his pistols bristled from the shelves. Randy's paints and papers cluttered a table in one window and in another sat a row of weary dolls, all recently outgrown, of course, but never to be thrown away. Still another sill held jars of different sizes, and in these were twigs or earth each concealing a spun cocoon or buried chrysalis. These, too, were Oliver's. Low bookshelves lined the walls, and above them, even to the ceilings, were pasted yellowing strips from ancient newspapers and journals, put there years and years ago by other children in another family. . . .

"Beet. Quint. A," read Randy, from the adhesive labels. "Beet. Symp. 3. Ero., Beet. Symp. 6. Pas., Schub. Trio E. Honestly, these records are in a mess. Schub shouldn't be in with Beet like that. The Beets should be alone together. Oh, here! Oh, *here* it is! Beet. Emp. Conc! But—oh, no. Oh, darn. The one below's an album of Bing Crosby and the one above it's 'Peter and the Wolf'! Gee whiz. And it was such a good idea."

"Heck," said Oliver, also crestfallen.

"Well, I know what I'm going to do," said Randy after a discouraged silence. "I'm going to write to Father tonight and ask him for a list of well-known emperors. It's the only thing."

"Send it air mail," said Oliver. "Now let's put on good old 'Peter and the Wolf.' Last time I heard it was when I was seven years old on a day that was raining and I had a stomach ache and Cuffy was away in Braxton."

Father's letter in reply to Randy's came four days later. "Here they are," said the letter. "But why?"

"Look," said Randy. "They're all divided up in bundles: Roman emperors and then Byzantine; Holy Roman Empire ones and French (only two of them, of course), and then the Hapsburgs. No Chinese, though. He must have forgotten them."

"Start with the Romans, they were the ones who thought it up," said Oliver, methodical as always.

"All right. So first there's Augustus, then Tiberius; then come Caligula and Claudius and Nero and Galba and Otho and Vitellius and Vespasian and Titus—oh, *Titus!*" screamed Randy.

"Titus!" screamed Oliver.

The emperor's namesake was revealed, at last, as their dear fat neighbor, Mr. Jasper Titus, Oliver's favorite person.

"Well, *I* never knew there was an emperor named that," said Oliver. "But I think you should have, Randy."

"I think so, too. I learned about him once," she admitted sheepishly. "I don't know how I could have forgotten."

By this time, naturally, without even discussing it, they were putting on their jackets and soon were on their way to call on Mr. Titus.

"It's probably somewhere in that old-fashioned clock he's got in the hall; the grandfather one."

"But that clock doesn't work," Oliver objected "It just stands there without doing anything, the hours don't even tell their names and go; *that* clock just always tells the world it's three fifteen."

"Poetic license," Randy said. "Maybe the very fact that it's stopped is what they mean about a voice being silenced long ago."

" '*Above,* a voice was silenced—' " quoted Oliver.

"Whoever heard of a clock that had its machinery on top?"

"Anyway we can just look at it," said Randy soothingly. "And he must have other clocks."

They knew better than to approach Mr. Titus's front door; that one was never opened. The whole activity of his house centered about the kitchen and back yard: kittens played there, ducks quacked and gabbled, and one red rooster crowed and strutted with three stout wives to praise him. Chrysanthemums were blooming in their bed, top-heavy and bending, and the last blue morning-glories, since the day was grey, were still wide open.

"Come in, come in!" said Mr. Titus. He was wearing a blue-checked apron and had a spoon in his hand. "I was just mixing up a batch of cookies, and I need eaters for 'em. Think you can oblige?"

Randy and Oliver assured him that they would make every effort to accommodate him and stepped with pleasant anticipation into the kitchen; they knew the cookies would be delicious: the two consuming interests of Mr. Titus's life were fishing and cooking, for both of which he had great talent.

It was right that the kitchen should be the heart and soul of his house. It was a wonderful room with windows facing south, many large ornamental calendars on the wall, and a stove as big and black and polished as a concert grand piano. The oven door of this splendid object was modestly embossed with its name: Heart of

Perfection. On the red oil cloth of the kitchen table there was always a tumbler full of flowers: nasturtiums or moss roses or petunias; anything the old man had happened to grab out of his tangled garden to stick in amongst the mint and chives and parsley that he kept there. Today there were some dark red raggedy chrysanthemums, picked too short, and a sprig of basil. Under the table the cat-basket was empty; before long Mr. Titus's cat, Battledore, would bring more kittens to it; her last ones had grown up and gone off to seek their fortunes. His dog, Hambone, lay beside the splendid stove, which crackled lustily as it devoured its coal fire. Hambone was really old, much older than Isaac, and instead of getting up when the children came in he lay where he was, looked at them, and whacked the floor with his tail.

"Him and me we feel the damp at our age," said Mr. Titus. "Hard to get up, hard to lay down; harder to set. The joints, they get corroded, just like old pipes. But then I never hankered much after exercise. Have a seat, have a seat."

Randy sat on the good old rocker with its flattened cushion and Oliver crouched on a footstool. Both of them had noted instantly that, though there was a clock on the shelf by the window, it was just an old-fashioned alarm clock, and above it hung the bird cage which housed Tibbet, the canary. He was yeeping away at the top of his lungs; goodness knows *his* voice was never silent except when he was sleeping, so it couldn't be that clock. . . . Pretty soon—after the cookies, perhaps—one of them would ask to examine the grandfather clock in the hall.

Mr. Titus sat at the table spooning cookie batter out of an old crockery bowl onto an old work-scarred cookie sheet. Everything about the place was old: owner, dog, stove, utensils. Tibbet was not young. Even the calendars were venerable, some going back as far as fifteen years. The current one was hung inside a cupboard door. "Don't like the picture on it," Mr. Titus explained. "I like a calendar with a real nice scene on it; moonrise on the water, maybe, or an Indian in a canoe. These young women they got on 'em nowdays—all dressed up in bathing suits and cowboy outfits and all grinning—they don't appeal to me."

"That's what I like about this place," said Oliver frankly. "Everything in it is good and old. It makes you feel comfortable. I like oldness."

"Everything's pretty antique all right," agreed Mr. Titus. "I bought this cookie sheet in nineteen seventeen. This bowl, this same *bowl*, I used to lick the leavin's of the icin' out of when I was a boy no bigger'n Oliver. My Aunt Effie's bowl, it was."

"In our house things don't last so long," said Randy. "They break or wear out or the dogs chew them. They get bent or lost, and sometimes they turn up in queer places. We found the eggbeater, after searching for days, in with Oliver's chemical set."

"I was doing an experiment," Oliver explained.

"I wanted to see what would happen if I beat an egg or two in with some iron sulphide, just for fun."

"What happened was a smell," said Randy. "Oliver lost interest in this experiment and let it stand there for a week, and pretty soon the smell began to put out feelers like an octopus, and they had such strength that they dragged us up the stairs to where they were coming from, and that's how we found the eggbeater."

"Yes, but another time, Mr. Titus—this was neat—Cuffy couldn't find her umbrella anywhere. Nobody could find it," Oliver said. "I did, finally. It was up in a tree, opened out nice and tied to a branch. Randy'd put it up over a robin's nest once when it was raining; she thought the mother robin would appreciate a roof. She didn't though; she and the father robin were insulted. They went away and built a new nest on Willy's window sill."

"That was when I was much, much younger," said Randy.

"Year before last, it was," said Oliver. "And, my, was Cuffy burned! Just as burned as she was about the eggbeater, and about the time she found the kitchen clock down by the pool——"

"That was when Rush was having the Turtle Derby; yes, and speaking of clocks, Mr. Titus," Randy cut in, with what she considered great presence of mind, "that grandfather clock in the hall must be a real antique, isn't it? I'd like to look at it again——"

"It's old enough, I guess. Been in the family for

generations. I let it run down years ago, though. The way it ticked, so slow and serious, why you could hear it all through the house at night. Made me nervous. Kept my conscience wakeful. So I just let 'er run down and slept much better after. Take this one, though," Mr. Titus nodded his head in the direction of the old alarm clock under Tibbet's cage (the Melendys glanced at it perfunctorily). "This one sounds real businesslike and hearty. Had it twenty years. Keeps good time, but the bell don't work any more. Gave up. Never could rouse me. . . . Well, what's the matter, Randy? You feeling all right?"

" 'Above, a voice was silenced long ago,' " quoted Randy, rising slowly to her feet in a sort of trance, like Lady Macbeth.

" 'Beneath, the hours tell their names and go,' " yelped Oliver, leaping up from the footstool and beating her to the clock.

Under the metal caplike bell on top of the clock was wedged the precious slip of blue, tightly folded and well-concealed.

"How in time did *that* get there?" demanded Mr. Titus. "Here, now, what *is* that?"

"Mr. Titus darling," said Randy, "please forgive us if we can't tell you for a while; it's meant for us, part of a secret kind of game that we aren't allowed to talk about. Someone must have hidden it there when you weren't watching. Has any of our family been to see you besides us? Before they went away? Rush, for instance?"

"Why, Rush was here, sure, just before he left, and so was Mark and Mona, too. Cuffy she's been by two or three times, and some of your friends, besides; Daphne and David Addison, and Pearl and Peter Cotton. Willy visits pretty regular; but I haven't seen your daddy since the summer."

"We haven't either," said Randy, saddened temporarily; but the thought of the clue revived her spirits. "Well, please excuse us, now, but I'm afraid we must be going."

"What! Before I take the cookies out! You can't go now before you've even et *one!*"

They saw that he was really a little hurt; and the delicate warm scent of spice that now pervaded the kitchen was certainly delicious. They sat down willingly, but when the cookies were cool enough to eat it was found that excitement had impaired their appetites. Oliver could only manage seven, and Randy came close to choking on her fifth.

"All right then, run along," said Mr. Titus resignedly. "Only soon as you can, you tell me all about it, now. I may be gettin' on in years, but far as I can see the human curiosity don't age a day. I want to know!"

"We promise," they said.

As soon as they were out of earshot Oliver handed the clue to Randy. "Read it," he said.

"All right. Listen:

"Sing a song of sixpence,
  A pocketful of gold,
A treasure trove in springtime,
  Worthless in the cold.
Start from your doorstep
  Faces turned west,
Up the wooded hillside,
  Over its crest.
Down among the giant stems,
  Down across the glen,
To where the cattle feed and browse,
  And uphill again.
Find a prelate in a pail,
  A crown upon a tree,
Find the garden of a nymph,
  And there find me."

Oliver was disgusted. "They forget I'm only nine years old," he said. "I don't know what a prelate is. What is a prelate, anyway?"

"A religious person, a dignitary of the church, I *think*. We'll look it up when we get home."

"And where in heck are there any nymps around Carthage? Or Braxton either? I'd like to know."

"It's a figure of speech," said Randy. "At least I guess so. Now, goodness, we'll have to look up all the *nymphs* there ever were. Just after going through all those emperors, too."

"Maybe we won't have to. This one does seem to

give pretty good directions at least. 'Up the wooded hill-side' and 'faces turned west,' and all that."

"Sounds like a good long trek, too," said Randy. "We'll have to wait till Saturday again. Gee whiz. It's tantalizing. I wish I could write to Rush and ask his advice about all this, but we have to keep it secret, and anyway I bet Rush planted the things himself. Who else in the world would have thought of Mr. Titus's alarm clock?"

It was growing dark. A cold breath rose from the fields and ditches. The crows sounded lonesome flying home.

"It's an awful long way off to summer," Oliver said.

"But it's only thirty-three days to Thanksgiving, and they'll all be home! And after that it's only thirty-one to Christmas, and they'll be here a long time then."

"All my children are going to be taught at home," said Oliver, and Randy agreed that she had decided on this course for *her* family, too. "But you're still here at least, thank goodness," she said. "Imagine if there was only one of us!"

Oliver had occasion to remember this remark when the next Saturday arrived.

CHAPTER V

A Pocketful of Gold

Sing a song of sixpence,
   A pocketful of gold,
A treasure trove in springtime,
   Worthless in the cold.
Start from your doorstep
   Faces turned west,
Up the wooded hillside,
   Over its crest.
Down among the giant stems,
   Down across the glen,
To where the cattle feed and browse,
   And uphill again.

Find a prelate in a pail,
    A crown upon a tree,
Find the garden of a nymph,
    And there find me.

THE NEXT Saturday Randy woke up without any voice. She did not know it at first. She got out of bed, went into the bathroom, brushed her teeth, and turned on the water for her bath. Vigorously running bath water always caused Randy, as it does nearly everyone, to wish to sing. But now when she opened her mouth preparatory to a vigorous rendering of "Oh, what a beautiful morning," no voice came forth. It was disconcerting. She turned off the bath water just to be sure, tried again, gave it everything she had, and succeeded in producing only a sort of whispery squawk.

"Laryngitis," whispered Randy disgustedly. She had had it once before, long ago. "Wouldn't you just know I'd get it on a Saturday!" She peered anxiously into the mirror; but one thing about laryngitis is that it doesn't show. She looked remarkably healthy. Saturday, she thought: the search for the clue, and now if Cuffy finds out, she'll keep me in all day and maybe in bed! Cuffy mustn't find out, that's all, I'll just have to be terribly careful.

She took her bath, dressed, and went downstairs feeling nervous and slightly guilty.

"Hi," said Oliver looking up from a king-sized bowl

of cereal. "You sure slept long enough. I've been up since six."

Randy yawned as though still drugged with slumber and not interested in conversation.

"She needs her sleep. She's growing," Cuffy said. "I declare I think she must have grown a yard this year. They measured you yet at school, Randy?"

Luckily Randy was saved from having to answer this question by a sudden shrill whistle from the kitchen kettle which always took this hysterical method of proclaiming that the water was now boiling. Cuffy hurried into the kitchen to catch it before it literally blew its top, or rather its whistle-spout, wildly into the air.

"Oliver!" whispered Randy urgently.

"Hunh? What are you whispering for? Why don't you talk out loud?" asked Oliver in clear full tones.

"Sh-h-h," hissed Randy, fierce as a cobra. "I can't, that's why. I've got laryngitis, and my voice is gone. If Cuffy finds out she won't let me out of the house, and I won't be able to go clue hunting. Help me, will you? If she asks many questions, think of something! Do something!"

"Well, gee, I'll try."

Cuffy came back into the dining room with the coffeepot and a platter of bacon and eggs. "You young ones! Always whispering! Such conspiracies and secrets." She sat down comfortably. "And what, if I may ask, are you two going to do today?"

"Oh, well, I guess we'll go out," said Oliver lamely. "Just go out or something."

"That's a good comprehensive answer," said Cuffy dryly. "That way I get a real vivid picture of the day's activities. Randy, why aren't you eating your oatmeal?"

"She is," said Oliver hastily. "She's eating it now, Cuffy, see?" And it was true that Randy had suddenly begun to devour the oatmeal with wild haste. She did not care much for oatmeal, she never had, but Cuffy was firm in her belief that the consumption of large quantities of old-fashioned porridge would help to build a noble character.

"You don't need to take it quite so fast, Randy. This is Saturday, you know; there's nothing to hurry for."

"There's everything to hurry for on *Saturday*," argued Oliver. "There's just one Saturday in the week. The schooldays could all be each other: they could all be Monday or Thursday or something, but Saturday is different and all by itself. So is Sunday; but Saturday's best."

"I——" began Randy; but stopped herself in time, turning the queer, croaking whisper into a cough. She had been about to argue that the days of the week all seemed different to her; they had different colors, even. Monday was blue, for instance; Tuesday was yellow, Wednesday red, and so on.

"Have you written to your brothers and sister this week, Randy?" asked Cuffy.

"*I* have," said Oliver quickly. "I wrote one letter and copied it off to each of 'em. I told about the Northern lights and the Regalis cocoon and Willy's bunion——"

"Yes, my lamb, I know. I helped with the spelling, remember? But you, Randy, did you get around to it?"

Randy smiled and nodded her head.

"Well, that's good. Here Randy, honey, here's your eggs and bacon. My what a lovely day! What a lovely long fall we're having. Means a cold winter they *say*."

Cuffy sipped her coffee slowly and luxuriously: she held the cup between her two plump hands and stared dreamily over the edge of it through the steam. Randy ate industriously, not daring to look up for fear of bringing on more questions.

"I'm glad you children are taking advantage of the weather. Out all day, that's the best thing. Who are you going to play with? The Cottons? Daphne Addison? How *is* Daphne, anyway?"

"She's fine," said Oliver at once, though Daphne was more Randy's friend than his, and he had not seen her in a month.

"That's good, she's a nice girl. Randy, more toast?"

Randy smiled again and shook her head.

"Matter? Cat got your tongue? Well, you've had enough, I guess," said Cuffy.

"Can we please be excused?" cried Oliver, his eyes shining: for the ordeal was nearly over, they had all but won. "We'll go straight out and do the dishes," he said with unusual alacrity, for though the children always did the dishes on Saturday, Oliver's heart was never in the project, and he had a quiet, efficient way of drifting out of earshot immediately after breakfast.

"All right, skedaddle," said Cuffy. "I think I'll just sit here and have another cup."

"Yes, do," said Oliver enthusiastically. "You just take your time, Cuff."

"We did it!" whispered Randy when they were in the kitchen.

"Well, just about," said Oliver cautiously.

Randy ran the water, full force, into the dishpan and shook out a huge extravagant cloud of soap flakes. Both children sneezed. Randy washed with a great clatter and clinking, and Oliver sang noisily as he dried and put away, to cover up the lack of conversation for Cuffy's ears.

It was going to be a fine day: sunny, and there was no wind; a fine day for clue hunting. If Randy could have joined Oliver in song she would have.

Cuffy struck open the kitchen door unexpectedly.

"Heavenly day, the *racket*—I been *calling*! Randy, Pearl Cotton's on the phone for you."

Randy stared at her mutely. Oliver, too. He could not help now.

"Am I a Gorgon? Are you turned to stone, or what? Pearl's still waiting, you know."

"I can't talk to her," whispered Randy.

"Why not, honey? What's the matter? Did you

quarrel? Are you worried? Tell me," said Cuffy, all concern, letting the door flap and coming to Randy.

"Oh, no, it's just that I plain can't *talk*," whispered Randy.

"Laryngitis," said Oliver glumly. The game was up.

In no time at all Randy found herself in bed with Vicks ointment on the outside of her throat and an aspirin tablet going down the inside of it. (Oliver finally remembered to inform poor patient Pearl Cotton of the turn of events.)

"But I feel *fine*," Randy whispered rebelliously. "It doesn't hurt or anything."

"Bed's the place for you," said Cuffy unswervingly, and in bed Randy stayed.

Oliver came up to see her. "We'll wait till next week," he said.

"No, you must go. Next Saturday may be rainy; we can't take chances. You must go alone."

"I'm kind of dumb," said Oliver humbly. "I don't see how I'll ever find it by myself. I don't know anything about nymps."

"You're not dumb at all. You've caught onto these things quicker than I have most of the time. The dictionary says a nymph is 'a youthful female nature divinity.' Remember?"

"I don't know how to tell one if I see one," said Oliver.

"Oh, it's not literal. It's probably someone with a

nymph's *name,* or something. You'll find out; you're smart."

Oliver left reluctantly, and Randy lay back on her pillows somewhat tired from this show of good sportsmanship and sisterly encouragement. "Well, I hope he finds it. Yes, I *really* do!" she whispered to herself defiantly.

Oliver decided to take his lunch along with him, and after a brief verbal tussle with Cuffy (who believed almost as strongly in a hot midday meal as she did in porridge) was allowed to do so. At ten o'clock he set off, carefully facing west, and Isaac accompanied him in a haphazard, preoccupied manner. It was very warm for the time of year, almost as warm as summer, but the trees were nearly bare: only the oak trees clung to their dry purple and crimson foliage. A late swallowtail dipped and rested on the air. "Brother, you nearly missed the boat," said Oliver. The butterfly ignored him, lilting off through the sunshine as though it were July and every field in flower.

" 'Up the wooded hillside, over its crest,' " Oliver sang aloud. He started up the slope to the left of the house, shuffling noisily among the million leaves; Isaac snuffed and scuffed close at hand. Jays called. Oliver's progress seemed nearly as aimless as Isaac's. He found a few leftover wild grapes, ate a handful and spat them out; they were fermented. He paused to pull apart a rotten stump, waking up a beetle and watching with absorption the frantic scurrying of an ant colony. He wrote

his name with a twig on the creamy underside of a tree
fungus, talked back to a squirrel on a branch, talked
back to a crow in the sky; found a hickory tree and
gathered a pocketful of nuts, searched for a stone to
break them with and, when he had found it, squatted on
his haunches in the sun for half an hour, cracking the
nuts and picking out the kernels with a pin. (He always
carried a pin this time of year, for just this purpose.)

By the time he started to descend the other side
of the hill, it was nearly noon. He whistled to the dog,
but Isaac had deserted, bored, no doubt, by the lengthy
hickory-nut process. Oliver descended slowly. He had
not been in this particular region for some time—not
since May—and when he emerged from the woodland
at the base of the hill, he saw the "giant stems" to which
the clue referred. What had been small upstart weeds
in May had, during the summer, attained a mighty
growth, and were now decaying. Oliver found himself
in a wilderness of pokeweed plants. The great hollow
stems were far taller than he, eight or ten feet tall and
still hung with tattered leaves and broken berries full
of ink. He had no idea how large an area they covered,
all he knew was that there were hundreds of the enormous plants; and this dead, fragile forest seemed a little
scary, somehow. He whistled for Isaac again and called
him, but there was no sound except for the crickets and
the methodical easy breaking of hollow brittle stalks
as he pushed his way forward. Far away a phoebe called
sadly, and a noisy company of chickadees flew away in

fright as he disturbed them. The crickets were everywhere, shiny and nimble, and so were the spiders; autumn seemed to be the rush season for them: Oliver kept getting cobwebs in his mouth.

"How much of this is there, anyway?" he began to wonder after a while. He was growing tired of fighting his way through the papery jungle and eating cobwebs, and he was tired of being spattered with purple juice from the great wilting berry clusters. Pokeweed was poisonous he had always heard, and now with the stillness and the inability to see more than two feet ahead in any direction, the seemingly endless grove appeared rather sinister: a poison forest in some terrifying tale. Oliver was not often a prey to such fancies and, on the whole, was not easily alarmed.

"It's just that I'm hungry," he said aloud, addressing himself in a sturdy, sensible voice which made him feel a little better. "I'll eat my lunch in the next clearing."

He walked on, or rather tore his way on, until he came to a small open space where he sat down. Food always had the power to cheer Oliver, and he was delighted to see that Cuffy, besides tomato sandwiches, had given him two liverwurst ones (a food she disapproved of usually). She had also supplied a chocolate cupcake, and an orange to slake his thirst. Oliver sat quiet as a mouse among the stalks, eating and enjoying. The sunlight rested on his head benevolently; the dry leaves rustled now and then against the stems. Here in this little wilderness he was as hidden and remote as if he'd found a pocket in the Andes; no one knew where he was, no one would ever have guessed, and sometimes, for a little while, that is a pleasant feeling.

When he had finished his picnic, he felt lazy and lay down on his stomach for a while, watching the tiny earnest activities of ant and spider and scarlet cochineal bug. Among these the jerking crickets looked as big as cows.

An airplane humming across the sky—"A Douglas DC-6," said Oliver—brought him back to his own world, and he got up to continue his journey. The twisting, crackling progress began again, and the bursting berries splashed him juicily.

Still, he seemed to be getting nowhere and when, after an hour, he came upon many trampled stalks, he was certain that they were stalks that he himself had broken, and that he had succeeded, like the lost people he'd read about, in making a complete circle. He did not care for this at all.

"Dumb jerk, you should have brought a compass," he scolded himself. "If there was a brook to follow, even, or a tree to climb and get my bearings——"

He was beginning to be quite frightened, though he knew this was silly. He seemed to have been breaking his way through these hollow pipes for many hours. He remembered all sorts of stories about lost children; children who had been found only after several days with nothing to eat but berries. "But you can't eat pokeweed berries," said Oliver. "Even if they weren't poisonous, by this time of year they're *stale*." Supposing he had to spend the night here, trying to sleep, with all those dry leaves whispering in the dark, sounding like people, ghosts, *things,* creeping toward him? Oh, no, he would have to find his way out before then! He glanced up at the sun, wondering how much more time he had before the dusk began, and found that the sun was nearly out of sight behind the weedtops, sinking, naturally, downward toward the west. The west!

"Dumb jerk," said Oliver again, sincerely. He had had to turn his head and look over his shoulder to see the sun. He had been walking south, paying no attention to the fiery signal in the sky. " 'Face turned west,' dumb jerk," he said and felt a little better, knowing at least that he now was headed in the right direction.

The crickets were all at work, singing—Oliver knew that they didn't sing, they rubbed their hind legs together—but still it sounded like a long, spun-out wavering song that had no ending. He heard nothing else when he stopped to listen: no cows, no crows, no sound of airplane or of engine. It was better not to stop at all; better to crash and plunge and make the noise himself.

Finally, though, he had to stop, to get a gnat out of his eye. Standing there scared and tired and berry-stained, he wondered why in the world he and Randy had thought of this search as fun.

"Good afternoon, child," said a pleasant voice.

Oliver's heart bucked in his chest. His scalp tingled; he could feel his hair rising. The whole afternoon—the spooky paper forest, the being lost, the hours of solitude, and the clue itself, with its talk of pockets full of gold and crowns on trees—had all had an unreal fairytale feeling; and the little elderly woman he now stared at seemed part of the story. She was small and thin with big gentle eyes. She wore a broad-brimmed hat, a red sweater with heavily sagging pockets, and a flowered dress. In her arms was a stout bundle of branches studded with red berries.

"G-good afternoon," said Oliver.

"Well, I heard this trampling and crashing in the weeds, and I thought maybe one of Addison's cows was lost again. Came in myself to see."

Oliver was deeply relieved to find that this was not a witch or fairy—of course he had not really thought it was—but just a person, like himself, and he began to feel as free as he usually did.

"Even if I'm not a cow, I'm just as lost," said Oliver. "I'm loster. Can you tell me where I am?"

"You're in Corn Hollow," said the little lady. "Over that way's Carthage and over *that* way's Eldred. Which one did you want?"

"Well, I live in a house called the Four-Story Mistake, maybe you know it? It's nearer to Carthage than it is to Eldred."

"Why, yes, of course, I know it well. You come

along with me," she said. "My house is on a road that
joins up with one that goes right past yours."

"Oh, thanks a lot," said Oliver, with a sigh of re-
lief. "What kind of berries are those you have? They're
very pretty."

"Black alder," said the lady. "Every fall I gather
them to sell to the Christmas-wreath makers. They use
them in place of holly berries. I find them over there,
in the swamp."

"May I carry them for you?" asked Oliver, wishing
that Cuffy could hear this courtly offer. His companion
seemed pleased, too. She gave him the bundle, thanking
him, and they walked on in silence for a moment or
two. Oliver thought of Willy Sloper's definition of good
manners: "Just like the grease on a creaky wheel, or
liniment on a sore joint. Eases the rub, that's all; reduces
the wear and tear."

By now they were clear of the pokeweed wilderness
and walking across a stretch of swampy pastureland.
Oliver looked back at the weeds.

"Must be about a million of those plants back there.
I thought I was lost for keeps," he said.

"Yes, the rains this summer," said the lady. "I never
saw them quite so tall and thick before. In the spring
when they're tiny little shoots I come and cut them and
boil them for my supper; they're like asparagus then—"

"But poisonous," cried Oliver.

"The root, only, and later on the berries. A lot of

weeds are good to eat. Purslane's delicious in a salad."

"*That* stuff?" said Oliver in disbelief. Purslane persistently invaded every garden he had ever had: a mean weed, he thought, with many little fat stems that broke off in your hand when you started to pull, leaving the root intact beneath the earth. "I didn't think that stuff was good for anything but discouragement."

"Nearly every weed is good for something. Some for medicine and some for dye and some for food. Nettles are very nice to eat, cooked, of course, and sorrel makes the best soup in the world. A man doesn't really need to make a garden, at all, for the garden is already here."

"Well," said Oliver. He could not imagine eating nettles. Or purslane, either. Still, he was interested, and he liked his new companion. "My name is Oliver Melendy," he told her, as though making her a present of his name.

"And mine is Bishop," said the lady. "Louisianna Bishop."

They were ascending another wooded slope, and soon they came to a cleared space, a woodpile, and a sleeping garden, and in the middle stood Miss Bishop's house. It was little; just the right size for her, Oliver thought. It had a roof as steep as a clown's hat, and smoke was coming out of the chimney like a tall feather. In every window plants were blossoming and growing, and he knew that in the summer the garden must be a fine one.

"Come in, Oliver, and have a cup of tea," she invited. "And I've got a fruit cake here."

Much as he wished to stop, Oliver felt he had no time to waste.

"I'm on an errand for my sister," he said. "Kind of."

"Oh, in that case——" Miss Bishop opened the back door, took the branches from him and put them in a pail. Many cats rose up to meet her.

"These are Pawpaw and Trundle and Sammy and Aunt Belle," said Miss Bishop formally. "Tell me, Oliver, where are you going, on this errand?"

"Well, gee, I don't know myself exactly," Oliver admitted unhappily. "All I know is it's someplace to the west, and I've just got to get it done now, today, because I don't ever, ever want to go through that mess of pokeweed again."

Miss Bishop was nice. She did not question or exclaim at this peculiar information. "Come with me," she said. "I'll let you out the front door and you'll be on the road; it goes west. When you start back, you can just come back along it, past my house and down to the next road. Then turn right, and you'll be home in no time."

Her little parlor was cozy. The pictures on the walls were thick as barnacles, and everything had a cover on it: the upright piano, the round tables, the backs and arms of chairs. The windows were covered, too, with many plants that had fancy blossoms shaped like pocketbooks and earrings.

"Can I come back again?" said Oliver. "I want to look around," he added candidly.

"Please promise to," Miss Bishop said cordially. "I'll show you the collection of pressed flowers that my grandma made, and the moss-gardens I keep all winter. I'll make Sammy do his tricks for you."

They went out the front door and along the path to the front gate. Beyond it Oliver noticed that the mailbox, like several others in the region, was planted in a milkpail full of earth. The name Bishop was stenciled on its side. . . .

Oliver turned suddenly. "Miss Bishop!" he cried. "Is a bishop what you'd call a prelate?"

"Is a—why, yes, Oliver, I think so. Why?"

"Part of this errand for my sister—gee, thanks a million!" said Oliver, rushing through the gate. Then he returned. "Someday I'll tell you all about it. Okay?"

"Okay," said little Miss Bishop, smiling at him.

He was hot on the scent, all right. Thirty yards farther on he was not at all surprised to find a tin sign nailed to the trunk of a large oak:

Drink Crown
The beer without a peer.

Yes, he was hot on the scent; but it was starting to get dark, now, and where was the nymph? Where was the garden with the purse of gold? When he came to the Addison's mailbox he was surprised. They never entered that farm by the front entrance, always approaching it by a shorter way: the back road that brought them up by the barn and outbuildings where business was always going on between men, horses, cows, pigs, machinery and chickens. Oliver loved that farm and its activities. He was not used to the front entrance with its wire gate, neat white-legged mailbox, and two huge soft maples. Already, in the house, the lights were on. Someone was moving to and fro in the kitchen. Oliver felt lonesome all at once and a little discouraged; it was too late to go on searching. He had failed. Sighing, he walked up the path to the farmhouse door and knocked; he might as well stop and say hello, anyway.

Daphne Addison opened the door, releasing a smell of cooking and a lot of noise.

"Why, Oliver! Hello. Come on in."

She was a nice girl, Daphne; calm and rosy-cheeked and pleasant.

"I just was going by—" said Oliver.

"For heaven's sake, whatever for? *This* time of day? It's just about suppertime."

He followed her into the kitchen where Mrs. Addison was busy preparing the meal, weaving her way between the blocks and toy cars with which Alexander, the four-year-old, had littered the floor, and speaking encouragingly from time to time to Mitchell, the newest Addison, who was standing in his play-pen, morosely sucking the railing. All around the pen lay toys and cooking utensils of which he had wearied.

"Look who I found at the front door, Mama!"

"Hello, Oliver; stay and have some supper with us. I'll phone Cuffy."

"Well, thanks, I guess I better not. I've been gone all day."

"Where've you been?" inquired Daphne.

"Just walking around, I guess you'd call it," said Oliver uneasily.

"Walking around? All day? You?" Daphne was astounded. "Whatever for?"

"Oh, just for a change," said Oliver rather airily.

"I never heard of such a thing!"

"So then I came across your mailbox without knowing I was going to, so I just decided to, you know, drop in and see how you all were. How are you, Mrs. Addison?"

"Why just fine thanks, Oliver."

"How are you, Daphne?"

"Well, gee, *I'm* all right."

"How are you, Alexander?"

"Hunh? I'm okay."

"How's Mitchell?"

"Teething," said Mrs. Addison. "He's getting a tooth with four corners and it hurts him."

At that moment Dave came bursting in. He was the eldest of the Addison children and Rush's good friend. He had been milking, and smelled of cows.

"How are you, Dave?"

"Able to take nourishment, thanks, Oliver. Anxious to take it in fact. How are you, Oliver? Boy, are you ever a wreck! What have you been doing, throwing ink at yourself?"

"I got into a bunch of pokeweed," Oliver said.

Dave lifted Mitchell out of the pen.

"Hi, Bottle Boy, what's the news at the front?"

Mitchell, in his little red overalls, changed at once from a small somber onlooker to a loud, jovial baby, leaping like a salmon in Dave's arms.

"Well, I better be going," Oliver said reluctantly. (The Addisons were having homemade biscuits with their supper.) "Cuffy will be wondering——"

Daphne and Dave, still carrying Mitchell, accompanied him to the front gate.

The sun had set, leaving a stain of crimson and yellow at the horizon; above, the sky was apple green, darkening at the zenith to a powerful blue and set with a few large early stars. The two great maples, stripped of leaves, made complicated silhouettes against the pale green sky; and from the end of one long swooping branch something hung and swung, like an empty sock.

"What's that?" said Oliver, pointing.

"An old oriole's nest," said Dave carelessly.

A pocketful of gold, thought Oliver, stopping dead in his tracks. He remembered the orange-yellow flash of orioles in June. He turned to Daphne solemnly.

"Is Daphne the name of a nymp?" he asked.

"An imp? It certainly is not!"

"No, a *nymp*. You know, with wings and all. Grecian."

By this time, in his frantic need to know, he had begun to leap up and down on the garden path like a demented brownie. The Addisons thought he had gone crazy. He saw the total bewilderment in their faces and ran back to the farmhouse and stormed into the kitchen.

"Mrs. Addison, *is* Daphne the name of a nymp?"

"A nym—oh, a *nymph*. Why, yes, Oliver. It is—or was. The nymph who was turned into a laurel tree. In Greek mythology, remember? Why?"

But Oliver, his manners thrown to the four winds, was whooping his way out of the house.

"Dave! Dave! Can you get me that nest? Please can you? *Please?* I just have to have it!"

"First tell me why?" demanded Dave, not unreasonably, and Oliver was forced to launch into the same lame explanations that he and Randy had given to Cuffy and Mr. Titus and the others.

"Oh, so *that's* why they were so interested in that nest that day——" Dave stopped short.

"Who? *Who* was interested in it?" Oliver implored, but Dave just shook his head.

"Listen, brother, if it's a secret *I'm* not going to spoil it. Here Daphne, you hold Mitch. We'll have to get up to that thing somehow, and a ladder won't do; there's nothing to lean it against; the branch stretches out from the trunk too far. We'll try a table."

Oliver helped him locate and carry out a small table; still not high enough. In the end they had to put a chair on the table and a box on top of that.

"If I break my neck the treasure's *mine*," said Dave. Balanced on the wobbly structure he reached up, cut the twig from which the nest depended and dropped it down to Oliver.

"You're certainly acting queer," said Daphne. "All excited about nymps and old bird nests and walking around all day like this. What's the matter with you, anyway?"

Oliver hardly heard her; he was searching the nest, and at the bottom of it, sure enough, he found the fifth clue wrapped in a piece of wax paper.

"What is it? What have you found?" demanded Daphne, but Oliver could not tell her. "Later on I will, though, honest. Gee, thanks an *awful* lot, you kids, I never could have done it by myself."

"Well, I certainly think it's all terribly queer," said Daphne, somewhat crossly. She liked to be on the receiving end of secrets, and who doesn't? But Dave clapped Oliver on the back and said, "You'll do the same for us someday; help us along the path to fame and fortune." He and Oliver moved the furniture back into the house where they could hear Daphne questioning her mother: "What's a nymp, Mama? Why was I named for one?"

It was really late, now, really dark. Oliver jog-trotted down the hill clutching the oriole's nest; he was singing a song called "The British Grenadiers," and the black woods beside the road seemed friendly, not mysterious and threatening as they sometimes do at night.

In Miss Bishop's little house the window lights glimmered through a filigree of plant leaves; there was a smell of woodsmoke. It made Oliver happy to think that he had found a new friend as well as a clue.

When, at last, he burst open the front door of home, he felt that he had been away for days. Willy Sloper, on his way out with a bucket of paint merely said "Hi," and Oliver was surprised that Isaac—who had returned in his own good time, as usual—did not spring up to greet him; he only rolled an eye at him and moved his tail slightly, not even a real wag. John Doe did not even do that; he was in the kitchen, glaring at Cuffy who was basting a roast; from time to time he whimpered with greed, and drooled on the linoleum. As for Cuffy, she merely clanked the oven door shut and smiled at Oliver.

"My soul! Go take a bath! Guess you had a good time all right, didn't you?"

"Yup, I did," said Oliver, feeling slightly nettled at so much indifference toward a returned adventurer. "Where's Randy?"

"Upstairs in bed where she belongs. I don't want you going near her till we know if she's catching."

But that was too much. Allowing Cuffy to assume that he was on his way to take a bath, Oliver sneaked up to Randy's room. Nothing indifferent about her, at least.

"Tell me! Tell me!" she croaked, bouncing in bed, wild with impatience.

He held up the silvery, knitted nest.

"The pocketful of gold! Hooray! But who was the nymph?" she said.

"Daphne Addison, no kidding."

"Daphne! Oh, *Daphne!* Of course, of course. Gosh. I knew there was a nymph named Daphne. I knew there was an emperor named Titus. I knew those things, but I didn't connect them. Oh, it's just a waste of money to try and educate me. I ought to tell Father——"

"Here, read the clue," said Oliver. "Read it out loud."

"I'll have to whisper it. Come here. Listen:

> "I guard a secret or a prayer
> With equal silence. I am old.
> Peace is the jewel that I wear.
> Compassion is the wand I hold.

> "Land of the dragon and the cloud
> Gave birth to me; I left that soil
> And came away, serene and proud,
> To watch a good man at his toil."

"They get fancier, too," said Oliver. "Whoever it is, it's nobody in our family. We haven't any poetry writers."

"Poets. Don't be too sure," said——or rather whispered—Randy. "I used to think you could tell a poet like a policeman—just by looking at him. But after David Harthstone came to school and lectured—and he's a famous poet, Oliver—I changed my mind. He looked just like anybody; somebody's father or a man in a bank or anybody."

"I don't see anyone in our family writing stuff like peace is the jewel, and all that——"

"I know. It's hard to imagine. We talk mostly in slang and shouts, all of us. Of course, Mona does quote Shakespeare a lot; she knows miles of it by heart; maybe it's sort of gotten stuck to her, do you suppose? So that she's able to write poetry on account of the amount she's learned, or something?"

"I know the names of every plane this country is flying; I can tell you just about all the parts of a plane and I make lots of models, but that doesn't teach me how to fly," said Oliver.

"No, I guess it's——"

Randy never finished what she was whispering, for at that instant Cuffy struck the door open.

"Oliver!"

"I just came in for a second, Cuff, to bring Randy this nest. See? It's a oriole's."

"They always look like they're just darned together, don't they? Real pretty. Real clever. No, but Oliver, I don't want you getting ahold of this germ of Randy's. Downstairs to supper with you, now, this minute; the bath'll have to wait till later."

Oliver was glad to go to bed early for once. He was really dead tired and felt as though he had covered vast distances that day. Cuffy tucked him in. She was an expert tucker-in, too; she knew how to pull a sheet smooth with a single twitch, how to pummel comfort into an unco-operative pillow, and when she stroked one's forehead with her warm, sure hand and said with certainty, "Now you'll get a fine night's sleep," she made one feel comfortable and easy. Oliver settled down in his cozy bed and watched contentedly as Cuffy opened the window wide, picked up a few items from the floor (socks, a book on moths, a roll of Scotch tape, and some walnuts), and then looked at him searchingly, as she always did, with one hand on the light switch.

"You all okay now?"

"Yes, I am."

"Good night, dear."

"Good night, Cuff."

The door closed. The room was dark. Wind rattled at the shutters and stars looked into the room. Oliver smiled and snuggled down, and slowly, calmly, went to sleep.

CHAPTER VI

Peace Is the Jewel

I guard a secret or a prayer
　　With equal silence. I am old.
Peace is the jewel that I wear.
　　Compassion is the wand I hold.

Land of the dragon and the cloud
　　Gave birth to me; I left that soil
And came away, serene and proud,
　　To watch a good man at his toil.

RANDY DID not feel sleepy at all. She had slept most of the day, dosed with aspirin and cough syrup, and now she was wide awake. Turning on her light quietly, she reached for the clue and studied it again.

In a flash she understood it!

About time they gave us an easy one, she thought, and, putting on her robe and slippers, she went to her door and opened it. She stood there, listening. All that could be heard was Isaac, snoring on the landing. From Cuffy's room there was no sound, no crack of light under the door. She ventured forth on tiptoe, and each creaky board sounded like a firecracker to her anxious ears. When she walked bang into the hall chest of drawers there was a thunderous clatter, and she held her breath, expecting the worst. But nothing happened, thank goodness! Isaac rolled over, audibly, and began snoring on a different level. Randy went on, inch by inch, to Oliver's door.

The moon was shining into his room, and he was fast asleep, a smallish hummock in the bed.

"Oliver!" whispered Randy. "Wake up!"

"N-n-n-h," said Oliver.

"Wake up, wake up!"

Oliver put his head under the pillow.

"No," he said.

"Yes!" insisted Randy. This time she shook him and suddenly he sat bolt upright, staring at her.

"Whassa matter?"

"Listen, I know where the clue is! I had to let you know right away, too, of course, because that's only fair. You know Father's statue of the Chinese goddess Kwan Yin? The one that's in his study, always, by the typewriter? *She's* got the clue, Oliver! She's the Chinese goddess of mercy, and that's what compassion means; it means pity or mercy! Peace is the jewel and *compassion* is the wand I hold. See? Do you get it? And it says she's old, too, and the Kwan Yin is: Father says she was made in the Ming dynasty, and that was hundreds of years ago. Are you listening?"

"Uh-huh," said Oliver.

"Well, why aren't you excited? Come on, get up! We'll go down to the study now and find the clue. Hurry."

"I'm coming," said Oliver, and with that he lay down again abruptly, sound asleep.

"Oh, dear; oh, all right," sighed Randy. She had done her best, but temptation was strong; she knew she could never wait until the morning, and that she must go investigating by herself.

Stepping carefully over Isaac she started down the stairs. Heavens, how they creaked. Some positively groaned. Deep in the house—no doubt in the kitchen— John Doe heard the stealthy progress and barked his special nighttime bark: stern and gruff, an imitation of a mastiff's.

"Shut up, John Doe," hissed Randy, and he stopped.

It was terribly dark in the hall, black, but she did not dare snap the lights on. Moonlight faintly illuminated the living room, but not enough; it looked strange. The furniture seemed so unfriendly. She was glad to get to the door of Father's study and threw it open eagerly. Moonlight filled the little room; Father would allow no shades or curtains at the window. It was so much his room—it smelled, still, of his pipe tobacco —that Randy felt a wave of homesickness for him.

There stood the desk at which he spent so many hours, and on it the blunt typewriter buttoned into its raincoat. There was the rack of pipes, and the row of reference books, but where was the little statue that belonged beside them: the bland, graceful goddess who seemed always to be wafting forward from her cloudy pedestal? She was not there. . . .

Randy turned on the light and looked everywhere, under the desk and behind the furniture, but Kwan Yin who, as long as she could remember, had stood there on the desk was nowhere to be found. Had she been stolen? Or risen from her cloud and flown away? At that hour, in the silent house, it was easy to be superstitious.

Deeply disappointed, Randy turned out the light and plunged recklessly into the dark living room. There was nothing for it but to go back to boring bed and boring sleep with the clue and its guardian still at large. Randy's eyes were blinded from the lighted room she had just left, but she stepped swiftly, her hands out in front of her, sure that she knew the way. What she did not know was that Willy Sloper who for weeks had been touching up the woodwork in the house had, that very afternoon while she was sleeping, arrived at the pantry and painted all the shelves, first being careful to stack the Melendy glass and china on a table in the hall just beyond the pantry door. "Be outa the way there," he'd told Cuffy. "The kids don't use that door much, and if I left this stuff stacked in the kitchen, they'd walk into it sure."

Randy walked into it now. Swerving uncertainly in the blackness, she struck it hard, instantly releasing such a shattering pandemonium as never had been heard before even in that lively house. Dishes dashed to the floor and broke; teacups bowled across the rug, coming to smash against the baseboards; the dogs barked madly. Speechless with shock Randy stood where she was among the ruins, watching the upstairs hall light blare on and Cuffy come running down the stairs with her grey pigtail flying and an andiron brandished in one hand. Seeing Randy she stopped abruptly in mid-descent.

"You!" she cried. "Just you? I thought it was a thief or a whole lot of thieves! What in the *world* are you doing? Oh, heavenly day, look at the Spode teacups! Look at the Worcester platter! Oh, my soul and body! What —*how*—did you do it?"

"Just whanged into it in the dark," said Randy sadly. "Just didn't know it was there. Nobody told me."

"And so what were you doing down here in the dark with a cold at this time of night in the winter practically when you're supposed to be in bed and sound asleep without telling me?" demanded Cuffy incoherently and indignantly. "Walking in your sleep, were you? You never did before."

Randy was tempted to let Cuffy believe this was the case. It would have made everything so much simpler; but she had never really lied to Cuffy and could not do it now.

"I came downstairs to look at Father's Kwan-Yin statue. She's not there, though. Oh, Cuffy, I feel so awful about the dishes and cups, and I loved that platter, too. I'll only keep ten cents out of my allowance every week and you can buy some new ones." Randy was half in tears.

"Precious few Spode teacups your allowance would buy. It'd take all your allowances from now till your wedding day—why, child, your laryngitis is gone. You talked real normal just now! That's something anyways."

"Scared right out of me," said Randy.

"More likely the dosing I've been giving you. Now run and get the broom and pan; no use crying over what's been done."

They clinked and rattled among the rubble for a long time. "Well, anyways you missed the Wedgwood teapot," said Cuffy, with some satisfaction.

"And every single Woolworth plate," added Randy bitterly.

"Never mind. It's done with, it's over. But why in time were you down here looking at a piece of statuary, and *what* did you say about its not being there? Why, I'm certain—I'm *sure* I saw it there last week——"

" 'Tisn't there now," said Randy.

"Funny. Well, I'll find it tomorrow. Come to bed now, it's late. I'll bring you some warm milk."

But on the next day the Kwan Yin still was missing. "I just can't understand it," Cuffy kept saying. She was a fine housekeeper—or as fine a one as it is possible to be in a household beset by children and dogs—and it worried her terribly not to be able to find the figure or remember when she had seen it last. "Mr. Melendy thinks the world of that piece of statuary," she said.

Oliver slept late and no one woke him as it was Sunday. He came down at nine fifteen, hungry as a wolf, and indulged in a waffle orgy. Randy sat beside him to keep him company, though she herself was waffle-logged by that time.

"I just can't understand it," muttered Cuffy, wandering through the room in an aimless fashion quite unlike her. "I just can't understand it."

"What's she talking about?" inquired Oliver foggily through waffle.

"Sh-h. I haven't had a chance to tell you. I didn't get it; the statue's gone."

"What statue?"

"The Kwan Yin, silly. It's just vanished."

Oliver chewed steadily. "I know where it is."

"You know—you mean you *knew* last night that it wasn't in the study?"

"Why, sure. I knew it wasn't two days ago."

"And you didn't tell me so? *Honestly*, Oliver!"

"Why should I tell you? You never asked me."

"Don't you remember me coming into your room last night and telling you I knew where to find the next clue?"

"Course I don't."

"I *thought* you acted awfully dumb. You weren't even awake, for heaven's sake! Well, where *is* it?"

"I don't think I ought to tell you," said Oliver exasperatingly. "I sort of said I wouldn't."

"Oliver Melendy! Are you *still* asleep? The clue is somewhere about the Kwan Yin, and we have to find it. I told you so last night, but you weren't even awake! You've got syrup on your forehead."

"Yipes, what are we waiting for!" cried Oliver, leaping up as though stung by a bee. "We'll do the dishes later," he shouted to Cuffy and made for the door.

Randy followed him, jog-trotting along the drive.

"Where are we going, though?"

"Wait and see."

She was surprised when he led her to the stable. They went in, spoke cordially but absently to Lorna Doone, their brown horse, and climbed up the narrow stairway beyond the stalls.

"What can this have to do with Willy?" wondered Randy, for Willy Sloper lived very cozily in the little apartment above the stable, surrounded by pieces of machinery under repair, seed catalogues, poultry journals and detective stories, and seemed worlds away from any thought of Chinese goddesses. His radio, tuned up good and loud, the way he liked it, made his front door quiver in its frame.

"Harriet—I hardly know how to tell you—Gerald has been arrested," roared a mighty female voice within the radio.

"Oh, Myrtle, Myrtle!" cried an answering giantess in tones of horror. "I KNOW he's innocent!" Her ensuing gasps and sobs shook the whole stable, sounding exactly, thought Randy, like feeding time at the hippopotamus tank.

Oliver was interested. "What do you suppose Gerald did?" he asked. "Let's just listen and find out."

"I'm more interested in the clue," said Randy firmly, and knocked on Willy's door. The giantess was cut short in the midst of her titanic grief and Willy opened the door.

"Well, hello there! Come on in, come in!"

His living room was cozy; warm and cluttered, with a pot-bellied stove crackling busily and a coffeepot always on top of it. John Doe was gnawing a bone on the floor, and on the table, smiling remotely above the glue and plastic wood and harness, stood the little figure of Kwan Yin.

"I had to let her know you had that, Willy," said Oliver, pointing. "I just *had* to. I didn't tell her why, though," he added virtuously.

"Why, that's okay, Oliver," Willy said. "I'd'a told her myself. It was only Cuffy I was kinda, as you might say, avoiding. Wasn't nothing to it, Randy, nothing real bad. Last week, remember, I put a coat of paint on the bookshelves in your Daddy's study. First, of course, I took out all the books and stood 'em up in stacks, some on the desk, some on the floor. Then I got up on m' ladder to paint the real high top shelves first and some-how or other comin' down my heel swung out and caught one o' them stacks on the desk and it collapsed over onto the next one and *that* collapsed over onto this Chinese Canyon or whatever you call her, and doggone if she didn't just lurch off the dang desk and fall down. I felt like I could cry. I know how your Daddy values that Canyon. But when I got to her she wasn't so bad busted as I was afraid; just a little piece chipped off her crown, and the tip of her pinky finger. I thought well I don't hafta worry Cuffy none about this, I'll just spirit her over to my place and patch her together. So that's what I done, and lookin' at her now, honest, would either you kids think she'd ever been broke, even a little bit?"

"Perfect, Willy, she's perfect," Randy assured him. "And while you were mending her, Willy, did you find anything on her? A little piece of paper, maybe? Blue? With writing on it?"

"What *is* all this about looking for writing on people?" asked Willy, justifiably curious. "Writing on *me*, writing on this Chinese lady; you think we should have information printed on us, or something? Name and age, married or single? Something like that?"

Randy was too worried to be amused.

"No, but Willy, *didn't* you find a piece of blue paper on her? She hasn't got it now, that's sure."

"With writing on it?" persisted Oliver.

"No, I sure didn't—oh say, now, wait a minute— why, I do remember I saw something. Yes, when I picked her up off the floor, I saw a paper with some handwriting on it. Let's see, though. What did I do with it?"

"Oh, Willy, what did you?" they begged.

"Seems like I—I *know* I didn't throw it away—but I was pretty upset at the time and I—yes, *I* know, I just stuck the note-like or whatever it was into the nearest book."

"What book?" they cried in unison.

"Golly, kids, doggoned if I can remember. Might have been a brown book, or was it red? *Might* have been green."

"Oh, Willy, *can't* you remember?"

Honestly troubled, he closed his eyes, frowning and striving to recall the book.

"Just can't," he said at last. "Is it awful important?"

"Well, we think so," Randy said. "The Secretary of State wouldn't, or the President, but——"

"Don't you feel bad, Willy," Oliver said.

"We'll find it," Randy assured him. "We'll just go back and look in all the books."

"I feel real bad about it," Willy said. "That was a

clumsy day for me. If Cuffy's worried about this here statue, you better tell her I got it. I'll bring it over later and confess all.'

As they went down the narrow steps Willy's radio sprang into life once more. Another troubled giantess voiced her distress.

"Oh, Janice, Janice, *why* did you forge the check?"

The search was begun again that afternoon. It was a weary business: Father's bookshelves lined the wall. Deciding to do the thing thoroughly Randy and Oliver borrowed Willy's ladder; Randy sitting on top of it and examining the books on the two upper shelves, and Oliver sitting two rungs below her working his way along the middle section. Every now and then, when their reaching limit was achieved, they both crawled down the ladder, moved it forward, and crawled up again. Luckily, there was little in the books themselves to delay the search; nothing to glance at and linger over or wish to read aloud from books with such titles as: "An Inquiry into the Nature and the Causes of the Wealth of Nations," or "Income Saving and the Theory of Consumer Behavior." Almost all the books had names like that, and none of them seemed a fitting sanctuary for anything so frivolous as a rhymed clue on pale blue stationery.

"How can Father *bear* to read all this? I think it would be easier to read Japanese," sighed Randy.

"I guess he's a pretty intelligent man," said Oliver.

Their arms ached and their heads hummed with phrases such as "trade cycle" and "economic development," and the light grew dimmer and the dogs whined to go out and it seemed as if the clue would never, never come to light.

Randy paused unbelievingly to digest the title of one of the books: "Die Politische Oekonomie von Standpunkle der Geschichtichen Methode."

"Just listen to this a minute," said Randy, and wildly mispronounced the massive title. "Words like that sound like something you could build a house with."

"Or sock a giant with," said Oliver.

Nevertheless it was the pages of this forbidding volume that released the clue; the folded paper fluttered, like a blue butterfly, to the floor. Randy and Oliver fell from the ladder simultaneously.

Randy held the message up to the fading light and read the words:

"Now comes the hour to put the game away,
    And greet the joyous season of the year.
    The time of Tree and Star is drawing near;
Forget the search and revel in the day!

"P.S. In other words the search is suspended until after the holidays, when again a clue will come to you by mail.

"P.S. II. And remember, not a word to *anyone!*"

"The joyous season of the year," said Oliver. "What's joyous about November?"

"You know what *I* think," Randy said. "I think we've been smarter than they expected. We weren't supposed to get this far in the search till around Christmastime."

"It must be Mona and Rush and Mark who did it all, then," said Oliver. "Your own family always counts on you to be dumber than you are."

"I'm sort of glad it's over for a while," said Randy. "Now we can concentrate on getting ready for Christmas."

CHAPTER VII

The Joyous Season

Now comes the hour to put the game away,
  And greet the joyous season of the year.
    The time of Tree and Star is drawing near;
  Forget the search and revel in the day!

THANKSGIVING WEEKEND came and went, but it was too fast. There was no time to catch up. Rush and Mark kept talking about boys at school that no one else had ever heard of and roaring together over private jokes. Mona seemed almost like a stranger, so grown-up, and she had a new haircut (very short, with bangs in front) and openly used lipstick. It was not exactly like old times, and no sooner had they come, it seemed, than they departed, leaving an air of haste behind them. The house was much too large and quiet for comfort, and Isaac was homesick for Rush all over again.

One good thing, though: Father didn't depart.

"And I'm not going to for a long time, either," he said. "I don't even want to go to Carthage for pipe tobacco. I just want to walk around the place, and talk to my kids, and throw sticks for the dogs and eat everything Cuffy cooks."

It was wonderful to have him back. Every afternoon when they came home, they knew he would be there, to talk to them and listen to them and help them with their homework. At night he often read aloud for an hour after supper: old favorite stories like "The White Seal" and "The Five Children" and "Castle Blair" and "Tom Sawyer." If he was busy, it was still comfortable to know that he was there and hear the benevolent woodpecker sounds that issued from his typewriter.

So time, instead of lagging, moved easily toward Christmas, and suddenly they were all back again and there was time to get accustomed to each other, and home was home the way it used to be.

None of the Melendys ever forgot that vacation—in the memory of each those weeks had a shine and glitter that would never grow dim. For one thing the weather was right. December, unlike some Decembers, seemed to have modeled itself on all the Christmas cards in the world. It snowed and snowed, and when it did not snow, the sun came out and the fields sparkled as if they had been covered with granulated sugar. There was hardly any wind, so the trees kept their heavy epaulettes of snow, and the iron deer in front of the house wore big white mobcaps on their antlers.

"I keep expecting the smoke to come out of the chimney and form the words, 'Season's Greetings,'" said Rush.

The children were in and out of the house all day; nobody's galoshes ever had a chance to dry, and Cuffy just spread newspapers all over the hall and gave up worrying about footprints.

Outdoors the scene was a litter of sleds; Melendy sleds and the sleds of friends, whizzing down the hill-sides between the trees, or idle and abandoned on the snowy lawn. Mark and Rush and Dave Addison skied down the east slope (where there were plenty of good hazards), and even Willy Sloper took to snowshoes: he looked like a big web-footed duck as he tracked across the pastures. Oliver and Billy Anton got two dishpans and went spinning, toplike, down the south slope until they were dizzy and sick at their stomachs, and then they'd lie down quietly in the deep cold feather bed of snow until they felt well enough to start spinning again. The dogs had white beards all the time; and the air smelled very clean—so dry and cold that everyone's nostrils felt crackly inside.

Another thing that made them all extremely happy was the fact that Mrs. Oliphant came home with Mona to visit them; they were always glad to see the tall, deep-voiced old lady who was their good friend. Besides being an interesting person—among other things she had once been kidnapped by gypsies—she liked children, and seemed to respect them, so that they in turn liked and respected her. With Cuffy and Mrs. Oliphant both in the house it was like having two grandmothers, Randy said. "Two special, marvelous, made-to-order ones. Better than any real inherited ones that I ever saw." Undoubtedly her presence contributed to the joyful spirit that pervaded the house.

Indoors, when the day was over, there was an atmosphere of wild festivity. The Office piano tinkled and clanked and thundered under Rush's flying fingers, and everybody was always bursting into Christmas carols.

"The first day of Christmas my true love sent to me
A partr-i-idge in a pear tree. . . ."

That was all that Oliver could ever remember of the song, but it was enough to suit him, and he droned it over and over again accompanied by sniffles. His nose was always running from the cold.

Randy was haunted by "We Three Kings of Orient Are," just as she was haunted by it every Christmas, and Rush kept bellowing, "Deck the halls with boughs of holly," in his terrific new voice. Somewhere between

September and now it had undergone, and was still un-
dergoing, a change. When he spoke or sang it was as if
some new person, a stranger, had come into the house,
but he looked and acted the same as ever.

"And speaking of decking," he said one day, "we
ought to all go out and gather some deck-material from
the woods. Mark knows where to find holly."

This was the kind of errand everyone enjoyed, and
in a matter of minutes they were all back in their wet
galoshes and steamed mittens, and on their way along
the furry, muffled paths. They brought their sleds to
carry home the loot and also because it was probable
that they would find a good coasting place or two along
the way. The dogs bounded and floundered beside them,
and Mark led the procession.

It was one of the snowing days. The flakes came
down in big soft blobs like pillow feathers. The woods
were silent and transfigured.

But the Melendys took care of the silence; they
whooped and roughhoused and zigzagged and stopped to
coast. . . . Oliver found himself a house under the
bottom branches of a spruce; the snow had covered them
and bowed them down, and when he crawled in under
them, very carefully, he found himself in a little sweet-
smelling igloo. Flakes tinkled delicately on the roof
above, and he was very happy.

"Where's Oliver?" asked Mona's voice after a while,
and he sat there, close to the tree trunk, listening with
pleasure as they called and searched for him. When they

began to sound worried he came out and showed them his hiding place and after that, of course, they each had to find one. For a while there was a savage village in the woods, though whether it belonged to Huron Indians or Alaskan Eskimos, no one could agree. Even Mona joined in the game. She had come home immensely grown-up, but seemed to be dropping a year of her age each day, and it was much more comfortable like that. Nevertheless it was she who first remembered about the time.

"Heavens, kids, it'll be dark before you know it!"

"And the place is still about a mile away," said Mark.

They jog-trotted through the quiet woods until they came to a rocky hillside where the holly trees grew. They looked glossy as jet against all that white, and their berries were like coral beads, but they were very prickly to pick and a lot of shrieking and complaining accompanied the cutting of branches. Oliver just rebelled, though being Oliver he did not advertise it but simply withdrew quietly and began pulling strips of papery bark from a birch tree. He planned to write some letters on it when he got home; the Indian spirit was in his blood.

By the time they had all the holly they needed, and all the laurel and long boas of ground pine, the light was beginning to fade. "We'll have to hurry or we might get a little lost," Mark said. He, after all, knew this territory better than any of them, having lived in it all his life, and they trotted obediently along behind him, single file, through the pearly dusk. The dogs had gotten bored and chilly and gone home ages ago. The children fell silent; they were tired and had made more than the day's quota of noise already. They could hear the snow, now prickling and whispering, and as the darkness grew the woods seemed strange to them and threatening. They were cold, too, and hungry; longing to get home.

Suddenly with a terrifying crash of underbrush something burst out of the woods to the left and just in front of them: a huge, wild, galloping thing! Mona screamed and so did Randy, and all their hearts lunged in their chests before they realized that the creature which had crossed their path and was now vanishing up the slope to their right was a deer.

"A ten-point buck," said Mark, in some awe. "And he just about stepped on my boot!"

"Too bad he didn't in a way," Rush said. "Then when people asked you how you'd hurt your foot, you could kind of yawn and say, 'Oh, a deer stepped on it in passing. They never look where they're going.'"

"Brother!" said Oliver. "That's the closest to a wild animal I ever was, outside a zoo."

The deer had broken their mood of silence. Rush, pulling his loaded sled, began to sing "The Holly and the Ivy," and everyone else joined in.

"Hey, we're not bad!" said Rush, at the end of the carol. "Especially now that my voice has changed and we've got a bass."

"I was thinking we sounded swell," said Mark modestly.

"Well, why don't we do something about it then?" suggested Mona, who did not believe in hiding any lights under any bushels. "Have a chorus or give a concert or something."

"Why don't we go carol singing on Christmas Eve?" said Oliver. "We could go and sing in front of people's houses, and they'd ask us in and give us cake and stuff." And I'd get to stay up good and late for once, he thought.

To his surprise this idea was greeted with enthusiasm by all.

"We never did it before, at least not seriously," Randy said.

"There are lots of people we could sing to," Mona said. "The Cottons and the Wheelwrights; Mr. Coughing. . . ."

"Mr. Titus," said Oliver warmly.

"Oh, natch. We'd never leave him out."

"Let's sing some more right now to practice up," said Randy. "Let's sing about King Wenceslaus."

Together they sang the nice, good-hearted ballad as they marched through the woods, Mark leading as if he were the King himself and the others treading in his footprints.

On Christmas Eve the snow was still thick on the ground, but the sky was clear and starry. The Melendys, at Father's suggestion, had borrowed back the team of

work horses, Jess and Damon, from Mr. Addison. They
also borrowed the big old-fashioned hauling-sleigh from
his barn, and two of his children, Daphne and Dave, to
help with the singing. Cuffy and Mrs. Oliphant refused
to be lured away from the warm bright house. "We'll
stay at home and welcome Santa Claus," said Mrs. Oliphant, busily tacking stockings to the mantel. "It's years
since I've met an attractive man of my own age."

Willy drove the sleigh and Father perched beside
him on the driver's seat, but the children sat in back of
them snuggled into the deep straw that filled the boxlike
sleigh.

"I feel as if I were Louisa M. Alcott," Randy said
happily.

"I feel as if I were the Countess Natasha Rostova,"
said Mona. "In 'War and Peace.' Russian. By Leo Tol-
stoy. A classic."

The sleigh bells chimed and jingled sweetly. Jess
and Damon jogged comfortably along the fluffy roads,
and there were so many stars in the sky that Oliver said,
"Aren't there more of them than usual tonight? Maybe
they add some extra ones on Christmas Eve. To cele-
brate."

"It's just because there's no lights around to inter-
fere," said Mark. "You can really get a good look at them
for once."

Carthage when they came to it, though, was a blaze
of lights. There was a huge dazzling Christmas tree on

Main Street, and a lot of red and green bulbs hung up above it spelling "Merry Xmas Folks."

Willy drew up in front of the Wheelwright house and the children got out. Father and Willy stayed where they were, for though Willy loved music he was tone-deaf, and Father as Mona had said, "is the most marvel-ous man in the world, but when he sings, it's more like buzzing."

"I feel awfully silly, don't you?" she said now. "I mean, standing right here on Main Street and singing all in a bunch with people going by."

"No, you don't, you like it," Rush said. "You al-ways love giving a performance!"

"And it's Christmas we're singing about," Randy reminded her. "It's not something silly or show-offy."

After a short whispered argument they began with: "Oh, little town of Bethlehem, how still we see thee lie." They had to sing it good and loud because there was nothing still about the little town of Carthage that Christmas Eve. But the music wove its usual Christmas spell, the passers-by stopped, and some of them joined in, and so did Mr. and Mrs. Wheelwright in the door-way; Mr. Wheelwright (one of Carthage's two traffic cops), just off duty and still splendid in his uniform. Even Father and Willy caught the spirit and got down from the sleigh and humbly added their share.

After more carols they were all shepherded into the little furniture-crowded cozy house with its dogs, cats and birds, and were fed with Mrs. Wheelwright's famous jelly doughnuts, cheesecake and strong coffee. (Even Oliver.)

Then, properly hugged and kissed, they went on to the Cottons', and then to Mr. Coughing's and the Vogeltrees' and the others. At each place they were welcomed warmly and fed. It was a wonderful night.

"If we don't hurry, he'll have gone to bed," said Oliver, at last, worrying about Mr. Titus.

So they all piled back into the sleigh again and covered themselves with the cold crisp straw, and jingled off along the lonely starlit road.

Mr. Titus's house was dark in front, but when they got out of the sleigh and tiptoed around the corner they saw the kitchen windows, warm and yellow, and in one of them, above the sash curtain, the old man's head, snowy as that of Santa Claus. He was working at something, wearing his spectacles.

"Sh-h," they told each other. Oliver started to giggle, he couldn't help it, but he stopped when they began to sing:

"God rest ye merry, Gentlemen
Let nothing you dismay. . . ."

Up came Mr. Titus's head, startled. He left his chair and now the kitchen door flew open. He stood there in the lighted rectangle, with Battledore rubbing herself against his ankles and Hambone wagging his old tail in the background. In his hand Mr. Titus held a sock; he had been mending.

"Thank you. God bless you. Merry Christmas," he said when they had finished. "And now come in, and we will have a party!"

There were delicious things to eat in Mr. Titus's kitchen: he always baked a great many pies, cakes, and cookies at Christmastime to give away as presents and just to have on hand.

The Melendys, though, were unable to do more than toy with these delicacies. All but Oliver, that is. Oliver went to town on everything.

"They all ate at all the places," he explained, with his mouth full. "But I didn't. I knew the best was coming last, and I saved up for it."

As they drove home, shortly before midnight, they were soon half-asleep in the cozy straw. All but Oliver, that is. Oliver had drunk a cup of coffee at each place (without drawing attention to it, naturally) and was as brightly wide-awake as any owl. He asked Father so many questions about the stars that Father finally begged for mercy. "I never knew I didn't know so much," he said ungrammatically, for he was very sleepy.

"Never mind," said Oliver. "I've just about decided that astronomy is going to be my next phase, anyway."

Randy, nodding between Mark and Mona, thought dreamily: No matter how good Christmas is, it can never be as nice as this has been.

And yet it was. All their presents were just what they had hoped for, no one quarreled or got a stomach ache; from beginning to end it was a perfect day. And after it there was another perfect week.

On New Year's Eve, Randy and Rush leaned out of the window and listened to the midnight whistles and bells from all the towns around: Carthage, Braxton, Eldred. Over and under these sounds they could hear the night wind in the trees: a year blowing away, a year blowing in.

"Happy New Year, Ran."

"Happy New Year, Rush."

Leaning there beside him she longed to tell him about the mysterious search that she and Oliver were engaged in. She hated to have secrets from Rush; but nothing could be done, her lips were sealed. She sighed.

"What's the matter? Thinking up resolutions?"

"I wish it wasn't almost over. I wish you didn't have to go back."

"I know. It's not so awfully long till spring vacation though; and after that till summer. And then we'll all be home again for months."

And the mystery will be solved, she thought, and we can talk about it. Anyway the clues are fun, and they'll begin again now.

"Come on," she said. "Let's go wish the others Happy New Year."

"Check," said Rush.

CHAPTER VIII

Prisoned in Ice

The search continues; luck attend the way.
I am the seventh clue and I am near.
Prisoned in ice, denied the light of day,
Rescue me quickly or I disappear!

P.S. And this means *quickly;* before Monday morning!

RANDY LOOKED at Oliver. He looked blankly back at
her. They were standing beside the mailbox.
Father's New York paper and the January bills were
held forgotten in one of Randy's mittened hands; in

the other fluttered a page of the now-familiar blue letter
paper.

The dogs waited beside them, breathing steam in
the cold air.

"Prisoned in *ice*," said Oliver. "Gosh, when you
think of all the ice around here. *Gosh*."

"I know. Gosh," agreed Randy; for it was still very
cold, the brook was frozen solid and so was every pond.
Worse still, two days before—the day the others had
gone back to school—there had been a mild spell, with
rain, and when the cold set in again that night a great
glaring crust of ice had formed on top of the snow.

"I mean it could be anywhere, right here or anywhere," objected Randy, kicking at the crust with the
heel of her galosh. "Why, we could search forever! And
it's Saturday already."

"Well, at least it's Saturday. We have some time
to work on it," said Oliver.

Gingerly they began making their way down the icy
road. It was really as much as your life was worth; even
the dogs kept skidding and now and then fell flat, spread
eagled, with all their paws splayed out; it embarrassed
them when this happened and they pretended not to
notice it. Randy and Oliver found it easier to walk on
the banked snow beside the road and bash their feet
down hard with every step to break the crust. It kept
them from slipping and made a very nice noise. The sun
was out, the snow was dazzling bright, and all the trees,
encrusted with ice to the last twig, were like trees made

out of diamonds. When the breeze stirred their branches they creaked and squeaked with a nervous brittle sound. Randy picked up a dead beech leaf coated with ice; when she pulled the old fragment off she had a perfect leaf made out of crystal, with every vein intact. It melted slowly on her palm.

"Ice everywhere," she said. "*I* don't know where to start."

"What did it say about the light of day?"

"Let's see. 'Denied the light of day' it says. So the thing's all frozen up in the dark somewhere."

"Maybe under the waterfall?"

"I suppose it could be! That's frozen solid, and in under those rocks it's probably very dark. Let's go see."

They stamped their way down the hill and across the blinding lawn to the brook. It was frozen and covered with snow, so that it looked like a path or road that nobody had walked on; the only way you could tell it was a brook was by the little dark air holes here and there, and a locked-in tinkle of water that sounded from within it. The waterfall, as Randy had said, was frozen solid; it was a thick festoon of icicles like mammoth candle drippings, and it was strong. The children tried to break off pieces of it in their mittened hands but it was too hard and thick and slippery. Oliver went and got a hoe and Randy got a hammer, and they chipped and hammered and got red in the face and sweated, and bits of ice flew through the air, bright as prisms.

At last the main body of the frozen fall was cracked across; then there was a tearing, rending sound as the great fragment broke loose from the rocky ledge where it was fastened. It came off in their hands, and with it, most unexpectedly, came the water that had been dammed up behind it! Randy and Oliver were suddenly and forcibly struck with a mighty burst of ice water, exactly as if someone had trained a fire hose on them. Oliver fell over backward, and Randy stood screaming so piercingly that the dogs began to bark and Cuffy came rushing out of the house with the eggbeater still in her hand and no coat on. As she floundered and skidded across the crusted lawn the children floundered and skidded to meet her, soaked to the skin.

"What in time have you been up to now?" wailed Cuffy. "How could you contrive to fall in the brook when the brook's froze solid? No one else could."

"We were just chopping off the waterfall," said Oliver.

"It turned ugly on us," Randy said.

"Chopping off—but *why?*" lamented Cuffy. "Why in the *world?* What will you think of next? No, don't talk, just hurry, now, into the house and change your clothes!"

As they slopped, dripping and shivering, up the stairs, Oliver said to Randy, "I guess it wasn't there."

"At this minute I couldn't care less," replied Randy, through a lively chattering of teeth.

While Oliver was changing his clothes he thoughtfully hung his wet socks out of the window. It was in the nature of an experiment; he wanted to see if they would freeze, and he was rewarded. That night when he examined them they were frozen hard as boomerangs. They were shaped like boomerangs, too, though when he threw one it did not return to him. Willy, somewhat puzzled, found it three days later, still frozen, in the middle of the lawn.

Long before that, however, the Melendys had changed their clothes, drunk the hot cocoa Cuffy forced on them, put on dry snow togs and continued their desperate search. They kept at it doggedly, looking in all the dark places they could think of where ice might be: deep in the pocket of each rotten stump, each hollow tree; under every overhanging boulder, into every crevice of rock, but they found nothing except a rusted Scout knife that Rush had lost the year before. By nightfall they were cold, tired and discouraged.

"I don't think this clue is explicit enough," Randy complained. "When the whole world is turned to ice all of a sudden, how do we know *which* ice? And when they say near, how near do they mean? As near as you are to me, or as near as Carthage is to home?"

"Heck, I bet we never find it," said Oliver gloomily.

But the next day, of course, they felt differently and tore through their Sunday waffles, mad to take up the chase.

"By the way, kids," said Father. "What happened to yesterday's mail? I never saw it, and there must have been some. There's always some, and usually too much, at the first of the month."

"Jeepers," said Randy. Horrified, she stared across the table at Oliver, and Oliver staring back forgot to chew; his cheek bulged with waffle like a chipmunk's.

"We had it down at the brook when we were taking the waterfall off," said Randy. "I remember I put the mail down beside me on the snow. . . ."

"When you were *what?*" said Father, setting down his coffee cup. "I wonder if everyone's children act like this? I always thought children just lived normal lives: eating, playing baseball, reading books . . . *not* taking waterfalls apart and mislaying their parent's mail."

"We better go look," said Randy wanly. "After we took the waterfall off, there was sort of a flood, and I don't know . . ."

Father went with them, and when they got down to the brook they saw that the fall was frozen solid again, and they found the mail all right, too, though somewhat scattered and all of it frozen fast under a sheet of ice.

"Look, you can read it just as plain," said Oliver happily. "Right through the ice you can read it. 'Mr. Martin Melendy, The Four-Story Mistake, Carthage,' this one says. And up in the corner it tells that it's from the Carthage Dry Goods and Confectionery."

"And here's one from the telephone company," called Randy, twenty feet away.

As for Father, he had gone to get an axe. "I never supposed," he said morosely, "that the day would come when I would be chopping my bills out of the ice."

After this somewhat dampening episode Oliver and Randy continued their search, stopping only to eat a hasty but tremendous Sunday dinner. But to no avail; they did not find the clue.

As they walked back to the house in the cold dusk, Oliver said, "Well, we've failed this time."

"Maybe not," said Randy. "We always seem to get it somehow or other."

"Not this time," said Oliver.

Father had gone out for the evening, too, just to add to the general gloom, and due to the pressure of the search they had both put off their weekend homework till the last minute, and there was a lot of it. Faced with the prospect they sat down dispiritedly to supper in the kitchen.

"More ice cream?" said Cuffy, at the end of it.

"No thank you, Cuff."

"Better finish it up now, it won't be here tomorrow, you know, I'm defrosting the icebox in the morning."

"Oh, well, a little more then," said Randy. "Why does it have to be defrosted tomorrow?"

"I do it every Monday. Always have."

Randy's eyes met Oliver's. He also had seen the light, and they rose from the kitchen table as one.

"If only she hasn't thrown it out!" moaned Randy as they opened the refrigerator door.

They pulled out first one tray of ice cubes, then another, and there, yes, frozen into one of the little square cells was a scrap of something blue!

"Break it!" cried Oliver. "Here, I'll get the potato masher."

"No, no, that would tear it. Put it on a tin plate on the stove and let it melt."

"Let *what* melt?" demanded Cuffy. "I declare, what *is* all this?"

"Part of the same mystery, Cuffy dear," said Randy. "Like when we searched your pockets that day and couldn't tell you why, and you told us about Francis Wellgrove, remember? It's not anything wrong, just kind of a treasure hunt, only it's a secret. . . ."

"It's beginning to melt!" said Oliver. "Cuffy, please don't mind, but would you just go away for a few minutes? Please, would you?"

"Well, I suppose. . . ." Cuffy cast a dubious eye at the melting cube on the stove and reluctantly left the kitchen.

The two children watched the ice dissolve into a little puddle, and then Randy, reverently, gingerly, lifted out the saturated paper on the pancake turner. She laid it carefully on the drainboard.

"Lucky thing they wrote it in pencil this time," remarked Oliver.

"Oh, naturally they would have thought of *that*. Listen, here's what it says:

"Number Eight's concealed in Number Ten,
   And Number Ten, though old, is always right.
Has traveled half the world and back again;

Touched Italy, touched England, and touched
    France;
Carried a load with strength, been known to dance.
Unpolished, down-to-earth, and none too bright,
    Still, Ten has held his tongue and with good grace
    Done all his share, and earned a resting place.
With other worthy objects he shall stay,
Retired with honor; never thrown away."

"What do they mean—Ten?" said Oliver.

"I don't know, but we'll find out," said Randy,
highly elated. "We find them *all* out. I think we're
superb!"

"Seems to me we're always finding out by accident,"
said Oliver.

"Probably most discoveries are made that way,"
said Randy, not to be taken down. "Columbus was looking for India when he stumbled on America. Isaac New-
ton had to be hit on the head by an apple to discover the
principle of gravity. Both accidents. As long as the dis-
covery is made, it doesn't matter if an accident reveals
it!"

She lapsed into silence, pleased with the sound of
her words. I think I'll write a theme like that for the
Yearbook, she thought. It's kind of profound; I bet Miss
Kipkin will like it. . . .

"Now, then," said Cuffy, striking open the swing-
ing door. "How about all that homework that hasn't
been done yet? It's seven twenty-five already!"

CHAPTER IX

Number Ten

Number Eight's concealed in Number Ten,
    And Number Ten, though old, is always right.
Has traveled half the world and back again;
        Touched Italy, touched England, and touched
          France;
      Carried a load with strength, been known to dance.
    Unpolished, down-to-earth, and none too bright,
      Still, Ten has held his tongue and with good grace
      Done all his share, and earned a resting place.
With other worthy objects he shall stay,
Retired with honor; never thrown away.

"I GUESS IT's a piece of luggage," Randy said. "One of those old trunks or suitcases that Father and Mother took abroad with them. Goodness, I think that's almost too simple."

"Why would a trunk be 'known to dance,' though?"

"Well, it's sort of farfetched, but you know the way they jiggle on a truck or maybe on an ocean liner in rough weather."

"Why would a trunk be called Number Ten, then?"

"Maybe there's a number on the lock or something. We'll have to see."

It was Saturday again, and raining. The first week after vacation had been a busy one at school, and Pearl Cotton had had a birthday party, besides. This was really the first chance they had had to start the search.

"Where do they keep the trunks and stuff anyway?" said Oliver vaguely.

"Some are in the cellar room and some are in the storeroom in the stable next to Willy's."

"Let's start with the cellar," said Oliver. He had a particular fondness for this place since he had been the first, when they'd moved here, to discover a room down there, full of ancient toys and trophies: belongings of the long-ago children whose father had first owned the house. In fact it was here that the Melendy trunks were kept.

The cellar was a cozy place that cold wet winter day. The big furnace was crackling comfortably, and the grating in its door showed a glimpse of fire like the grin on a jack-o'-lantern. Willy's old stubbed broom and shovel leaned companionably against the wall, the wood was neatly stacked, the coal all tidy in its bin. It was a model of order, and the storeroom beyond it was just as neat. (The Melendy children hardly ever entered these two places.)

The suitcases were stacked as neatly as the cord-wood and the trunks grouped together under a tar-paulin like circus elephants. Isaac's old carrier stood in one corner beside three electric fans which were hiber-nating through the winter.

Oliver breathed deeply, with a sort of proprietary pride. "This is a good-smelling place," he said.

Randy had removed the tarpaulin and was looking at the trunks. Nothing on any trunk said Ten, but as they were old and widely traveled, they carried other interesting information; labels from all over the world, some of them with pictures on them: the Bay of Naples, for instance, done in bright sunset colors, and the towers of Carcassonne.

"I wish *we'd* ever been taken to those places," said Randy enviously. "Mona's the only one that was, and she was so young that all she remembers is falling out of a high chair in Venice."

"Into a canal?" asked Oliver hopefully.

"No, silly, just onto some old floor. Look, here's one from Greece; it's got the Parthenon on it."

"It's the names of the boats I go for," said Oliver. "The S.S. Berengaria. The S.S. Carinthia. The S.S. Adriatic. Boy! All I ever was on was the Staten Island ferryboat."

"Me, too; and a few rowboats, but you can't count those. Well, I don't understand this Number Ten business. The numbers on the locks are all much longer and fancier, but we might as well look into the trunks anyway. You never can tell."

But there was no clue in any of the trunks. There was nothing much; just miscellaneous tag ends that had been left behind: some wads of tissue paper, some wire coat hangers, one brown sock. Oliver found a crumple of newspaper printed in the year 1937; the sporting section, luckily. He sat down to read the old antique baseball scores.

"That's not buttering any parsnips," said Randy, using one of Cuffy's pet expressions. "Come on, let's look in the suitcases."

"You look in them," said Oliver. "I'm busy. Listen, did you know Mel Ott was playing then? Why, *I've* heard of him."

But Randy, who was ignorant about baseball, was not listening. She had put the tarpaulin back over the elephants and now began to explore the suitcases. In one she found a penny and a toothbrush. In another, some paper clips and a bead ring that she had made a long time ago. "I *wondered* what had happened to that,"

she said, but now the only finger it would fit was the
little one. Funny, she thought, you never think about
your fingers growing, too.

In the other suitcases there was nothing to speak
of: dust, stray pieces of Kleenex, a pin or two. Randy
sighed.

"I guess the stable storeroom's next," she said.

Oliver left the yellowed paper with some regret,
and they ran up the stairs and out into the rain, first
grabbing their raincoats. It was a beastly day, the snow
pitted and melting, all the trees howling, and the sky
full of scudding ragged clouds. They were glad to get
to the stable and embrace Lorna Doone and give her
the sugar lumps they had snatched from the kitchen.

The storeroom above was not so cozy as the cellar
because it was not heated. Their breath showed on the
air. But since it was higher and dryer than the other
one, it was used for many things beside luggage. Melendy coats and garments hung shrouded in large moth-
proof bags like giant bats at rest. The hat boxes were
built up in towers. Father's old mountain-climbing
boots and his trout-stream waders stood in pairs beside a stack of letter files and a stirrup pump. There were
odds and ends of carpet which Cuffy was sure would
someday come in handy again, and many neatly piled
cardboard boxes with mysterious identifications written
on them in pencil: Sum. bdspds., Ex. wn. shds., Sum. slp.
cvrs.

In the midst of all, with a narrow path around it,

stood an island of luggage: suitcases on a foundation of trunks.

They went through the suitcases first. No success. And then one of the trunks played a nasty trick on them: it still carried a checkroom tag marked 10; and they were sure that they had found the clue's hiding place. But when they opened the trunk, it revealed nothing but old crib sheets.

"Why on earth did she save those?" said Randy.

All that remained was one little trunk: small, shabby, with rusted clasps. They lifted the lid and saw that it was filled with old family photographs.

"Look, here's one of you in your high chair," said Randy, taking it out. "Man, were you ever fat! You looked like a woodchuck!"

"And here's one of you with no front teeth. Grinning like anything, and no front teeth! Ugh!" said Oliver.

"Here, let me see. . . . Oh, I remember when that was taken! I was seven years old, and I lost both teeth in the same week. They gave me a quarter apiece for them, and I felt rich and elderly. . . ."

"Here's Rush wearing a diaper."

"Here's Mona—at least it says it's Mona—she's bald as a doorknob and Cuffy's holding her up in her arms. . . . Cuffy looks so different. Younger, sort of, and not so fat."

Oliver glanced at the photograph. "I like her better the way she is."

The clue was forgotten. The cold was forgotten. The children sat on the floor, breathing steamily, utterly absorbed in these different distant people who had been themselves. A million raindrops drummed on the roof; music from Willy's radio drummed through the wall.

"I remember most of these pictures," Randy said, "but I'd forgotten that I remember them."

"Me, too," said Oliver. "Gosh, did you really ever have a hat like that?"

"I guess so; isn't it peculiar? Why look, here's one of Mother. . . . I thought we had them all at home."

Oliver took the picture she held out and studied it: a young girl sitting in a rowboat, laughing at some vanished joke.

"I never knew her very well," he said.

"Oh, Oliver, of course you did. But you were just a baby."

"She was pretty, wasn't she?"

"Yes. Yes, now I can see that she was. But when I knew her, I mean when she was living, I never thought if she was pretty. She was just Mother. The way Father is Father. The way Cuffy is Cuffy. The way any grownup is that you see all the time and love a lot."

"I guess so. . . . Say, who is this guy?"

"For heaven's sake. It must be Father."

The boy looked very serious. He stood with his arms folded, gazing sternly into the lens of the camera. His broad-brimmed hat was turned up in front, his nose freckled. His knickerbockers were torn at the knee; his high-laced shoes scuffed. His stockings—"*Stockings,* mind you," said Randy—were badly wrinkled.

"He wasn't a very fancy dresser," she said, "and someone's written on the back of it: 'Martin Melendy, age 11 years. The prodigal returneth!' Well, well. We'd better ask Father about this."

She laid the picture aside, and they went on with their family research: pictures of themselves and their parents and grandparents and relatives, known and unknown; pictures of babies galore: babies in bathtubs and sandpiles and buggies; on laps and on shoulders and in unknown adult arms. After a while it was too dark to see any more and as the storeroom was without electricity, they shut the trunk and went back to the house in the rain.

"I don't think it ever was a piece of luggage," Oliver said.

"Probably not," Randy said. "All that talk about travel made me think so."

"Who ever heard of a trunk dancing?" said Oliver. "Being always *right,* too. Hey!" He stopped dead. "I bet it's a shoe!"

"Maybe. Gee whiz, *maybe!* Unpolished and down-to-earth, too. And holding its *tongue,* and all. But who wears size ten around here. Father? Rush wears eights, I know, and so does Mark. It couldn't be Cuffy or Mona or us."

Willy came slopping along in his slicker.

"Hi, Willy, how big are your feet?" was Oliver's greeting.

"Size twelve," replied Willy amiably. "My feet expected to support a larger man. They outdistanced me. Why?"

"We're taking sort of a—sort of a foot census," said Randy.

"Well, anything to kill time on a bad day," said Willy.

Father was in the living room, reading. He had built a good fire in the fireplace and turned on the lights. It was warm and cozy there.

"What size shoe do you wear, Father?" asked Randy, the minute she saw him.

"Eleven," said Father.

"Oh, dear," said Randy.

"Heck," said Oliver.

"Is there anything wrong about size eleven?" asked Father defensively. "After all I'm not a small man."

"No, it's not that. It isn't anything, really, just something I was thinking of," said Randy helpfully. She held the picture out to him. "Look, what we found. Why does it say that about the prodigal on it?"

"Good heavens, I haven't seen that photograph in thirty years or more," said Father. "I was eleven years old and had just climbed a mountain by mistake."

"Tell us," demanded Randy, flinging herself down on the rug beside the dogs. Isaac was steaming visibly;

he had been out hunting in the rain. Oliver preferred the couch; he sat slumped way down, almost sitting on his neck, a position he considered both comfortable and relaxing.

Father lit his pipe, or rather relit it (he seemed to light it as much as he smoked it) and began.

"Well, let's see. . . . It was a long time ago, as you can guess. I was spending the summer with my grandparents that year, I forget why, and they'd taken a place at Lake Nemesee for the month of August; a little blue, deep lake with mountains all around it. I'd talked Grandfather into letting me take my dog——"

"Hector?" asked Oliver.

"No, the one before Hector. Gus, his name was. I don't know why his name was Gus, but it suited him. He was a low-slung, stout, bowlegged dog with one bent ear. I loved him and he loved me. It was a bitter blow to us both when Grandfather refused to let him sleep in my bedroom. He always had at home; he used to lie down among the shoes on my closet floor. He had a good friendly way of snoring, and when he woke up to scratch himself the floor would shake. I missed all that, but my grandfather was unyielding. He did not approve of dogs in bedrooms. Gus didn't like it any better than I did; sometimes I could hear him give a long dismal howl of loneliness and boredom in the kitchen downstairs. I could hardly stand it. Grandfather could hardly stand it either; he took to shutting Gus out in a little woodshed back of the cottage every night.

"My grandmother was understanding, though. 'Never you mind, Martin,' she'd say. 'I'll just slip out and give him a bone before I go to bed. It'll take his mind off his loneliness.' "

"How *horrible* of your grandfather," cried Randy.

"He didn't realize. He was a fine man, and I liked him; he was a little elderly and strict, that was all, and didn't remember much about boys, being at that time the father of seven grown-up daughters. . . . Well, one night, full moon, it was, a big wind sprang up. What woke me was a door banging somewhere; it sounded as if it was outside. My first thought was of Gus, naturally, and when I looked out the window, sure enough, there was the shed door wide open, clapping and banging against the wall. I whistled for Gus, but he didn't come, and I listened for him, too, but could hear nothing, so I got out of bed and ran downstairs and out into the yard.

"But no Gus. I searched high and low, but never a sign of him. I began to be so miserable and worried and angry that I lost all sense of proportion. I ran back into the house and upstairs and put on my clothes. Then I ran down again into the kitchen and wrote a note by moonlight and left it on the table. It was a reckless note addressed to my grandfather and informing him that I wasn't coming back till I'd located Gus. 'Even though it takes me far afield,' I wrote. (I remember being proud of the phrase.)

"I meant it at the time, and started off defiantly,

down the road in the windy moonlight, stopping every little while to whistle for Gus. When I reached the end of the road I kept on going, through the woods. The woods ran up the hill, but I thought I'd heard barking up there someplace and I kept on.

" 'Gus! Oh, Gus!' I was shouting and—I confess it—crying a little; I was so mad at my grandfather and so anxious about my dog, and the going began to get tough, too: hazel bushes as high as I was, just about, and blackberry brambles that scratched me half to death. The moonlight fell in splotches in the tangle, and the trees roared in the wind up overhead. When I stopped to rest, I began to think about how wild and lonely it was up there so late at night, and suddenly near by there was a queer, terrible voice calling out! Lost, inhuman! I nearly jumped out of my skin——"

Oliver got up off his neck. "Yipes! What was it?"

"It called again," said Father teasingly. "And then again——"

"Father, you're overdoing it," said Randy, also sitting up.

"So then the thing came flapping out of a tree, big and soft as a shadow: an owl, of course. I'd never been so close to an owl's conversation before, and I didn't care for it——"

"Oh, just an owl," said Oliver, slumping down on his neck again.

"Try being surprised by one late some night in unfamiliar territory, and see how you like it," said

Father. "I'd been thoroughly scared, and I decided on a compromise. I decided to go back to the cottage, tear up the note, and wait until daylight to search for Gus. But that was easier said than done. I started down the hill in the direction I'd come from, or so I thought; but I must have been royally turned around, because after I'd gone downhill for a while, instead of coming to the road I found myself going uphill again! I didn't know where I was. I didn't know what to do. I just kept ploughing ahead, up and up, figuring that when I came to a clearing I'd be able to see where I was, get my bearings. I wasn't calling for Gus any more, either. I didn't care for the lonesome sound of my own voice.

"How that hill went up! After I'd been climbing for a lifetime, so it seemed, it even stopped being a hill and turned into a limestone cliff, and I climbed that, too, I don't know how, and still I couldn't see where I was, the trees were so tall. Up and up and up I went, and the wind died away and the sky commenced to lighten, and then I came to the top of the cliff and ploughed through another tangle, and suddenly found myself out in the open on a rough, tilted, grassy field, and every rooster in the county was crowing. I could see for miles! The sun was just showing the tip of its crown over the horizon. Far away below, and to the right of me, lay the valley I had come from, with its toy houses and churches and little toy lake. Tiny cows were filing out of barns on their way to pasture, and my grandparents' cottage—still in shadow as the whole valley was—looked quiet and undisturbed: no distress signals flying, nobody dashing out of the door, probably they weren't even up yet, hadn't even guessed that I was gone. I felt a little put out about it, though. Added to that, from where I was—high as I was—I saw a tiny little speck of white moving this way and that way around the house; it could have been a blowing paper or one of the neighbor's Leghorn hens, but I knew that it was Gus, come home in his own good time.

"My feelings were mixed. I was glad to see that Gus was safe, and to get my bearings; but still I felt I'd gone to an awful lot of trouble for nothing, and now there was the return journey to be done, downhill through all the vines and thorns and mean twigs again, to say nothing of the hazards of scrambling and slipping down the sandstone cliff. I'd had very little sleep, of course, and a terrific amount of exercise and I was dog-tired.

"By the time I staggered in at the gate, it was full daylight, and I found everyone just as concerned as I'd thought they should be. More so. I was thoroughly ashamed of myself when I saw my grandmother in tears and my grandfather about to set out in search of me. He'd gathered up a couple of the neighbors, too, to help, and there was Gus, wagging his tail in an ordinary sort of way, just as if nothing had happened.

"I was a sight to behold, as you can see by the photograph: torn and dirty. 'Where in the world did you get to?' they cried. When I described the high hill, and pointed to it, it turned out that I had climbed Mount Alfred, the highest hill around there—a mountain, really—without even knowing it; and it was considered a difficult climb.

" 'Climbed it by mistake!' one of the neighbors kept saying. 'Climbed it by accident in the nighttime. That's rich, that certainly is rich!' And he made me wait while he went and got his camera and then took this picture of me, just as I was, all stuck with cockleburs and sticktights. Later it was published in the local paper with a piece about me. What had been a piece of reckless foolishness turned out, most unjustly, to be glory as far as I was concerned! I didn't deserve it at all."

"But what did your grandfather say?" asked Randy.

"And what happened about Gus?" asked Oliver.

"Grandfather and I arrived at a compromise after that. Gus was allowed to sleep on a mat outside my bedroom door; that was as far as Grandfather would go, but it was far enough. I could hear Gus snoring, and he could hear my voice talking to him if he got lonesome.

"Then, years later, after Grandfather had died, one of my aunts came across the photograph in his desk with the words about 'the prodigal' written on the back in his handwriting. She sent it to your mother."

"Why didn't you ever tell us this before?" said Randy.

"I thought of course I had; but perhaps it was Rush I told, or Mona."

"I love hearing about when you were young," said

Randy, and for quite a while she forgot about the clue.

However, they were no closer to finding it than they had been, and though they went through all the luggage once again, just in case, and then through everybody's shoes, they never saw a sign of it. And weeks went by.

In the middle of February there came a day that should have been the property of April: mild and sunny and still. It smelled like April. Also by extraordinary luck it was a Sunday. Father cast a withering glance at his typewriter.

"Kids, let's get a lunch together and go exploring."

"Perfect!" said Randy joyfully.

"Neat!" said Oliver.

"But where are my walking boots?" said Father a little later. "Has anybody seen my walking boots?" he called plaintively over the bannister.

"Oh, dear, Mr. Melendy, did you want them?" cried Cuffy. "You asked me to have them repaired, don't you remember? The soles was wore clear through. Oh, dear."

"Never mind, I'll wear something else. I have another old pair of climbing boots in the storeroom, but I'm saving those for Rush. I can't wear them any more, they're only tens."

"I didn't know grownups' feet got bigger," said Oliver.

"Sometimes they do," said Father. "Mine did." And Cuffy took this opportunity to mention once again that, though she now wore sixes, her wedding slippers had been size three. For some reason she was terribly proud of this fact.

Randy, however, interrupted her. "Did you say *tens,* Father?"

"Tens!" echoed Oliver enthusiastically. "Hurry up, Randy, come on!"

As they flew up the stable ladder Willy, who was currycombing Lorna Doone, inquired where the fire was.

"In an old shoe!" replied Oliver, over his shoulder. Willy and Lorna Doone shook their heads at each other, looking remarkably alike.

In the old right boot the clue, of course, was waiting for them.

"It's been here so long it's dusty!" said Randy. "Honestly, wouldn't you think we'd have looked in these?"

"Never mind, as long as we found it. What does it say?"

"It's short:

"At midnight when the full moon's bright,
(One, two, three, and to the right),
    Explore a cave well known to you.
    (Remember cake crumbs: find the clue.)"

"We only know one cave that you can really call a cave. It must be that one."

"Yes, and when I was eight I had my birthday cake there, remember?"

"When's the next full moon, though?"

"Yipes. We just had one. Now we'll have to wait till March!"

"Randy! Oliver!" called Father from below. "Are we ever going to get started?"

When they joined him, he said, "What canaries have you two been eating this time?"

"No canaries, Father dear," said Randy. "This time it's only little crumbs of cake!"

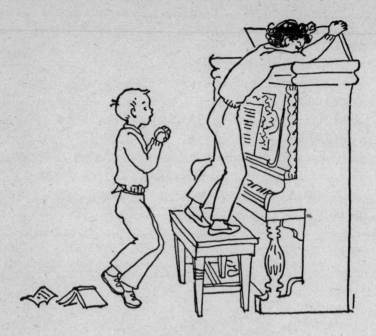

CHAPTER X

Explore a Cave

At midnight when the full moon's bright,
(One, two, three, and to the right),
  Explore a cave well known to you.
  (Remember cake crumbs: find the clue.)

"I DO WISH," said Randy, "that they'd stop giving us
clues that make it necessary for me to wake you
up. I'd rather rouse a dormouse."

"I'll wake up easy this time," promised Oliver, with a confidence not based on past performance.

It was the date of the full moon. They had planned and arranged for the expedition, and luckily the weather was with them. The late afternoon was clear and still and the coming night promised to be the same. They had their flashlights and some chocolate bars ("to keep our strength up," Oliver said), handily hidden away under the front steps, and Randy would again maneuver the alarm clock up to her bedroom.

"I'll wake you about eleven," she said, "because it will take a while for you to come to."

Cuffy seemed surprised, even alarmed, when they expressed a desire to retire immediately after supper. Father wondered if they were coming down with flu.

"We both feel fine," Randy assured him, "but we've done all our homework, and we just think we ought to go to bed early." (Goodness knows it was the truth.)

"Miraculous," said Father, "but I can't help feeling that there's something behind it all."

Randy smiled sweetly and kissed him on the brow.

The burring of the alarm clock at eleven was a horrid shock. Randy did not feel that she had had more than a moment's sleep and rose, groaning and reluctant, from her warm bed. Oliver proved just as difficult to wake as he always had on such occasions and was only brought to comply by a threat of cold water in the face.

But before very long they were on the way, gliding

along the moonlit road on their bicycles. "Thank goodness the snow's gone," said Randy. "We would have had to walk the whole way."

The moon was hard and bright, high in the sky. The stars seemed smaller than usual: tiny, flinty specks. Fortunately there was no wind; the bleak and leafless woods hardly murmured as they rode between them. The two bicycle lights wavered along, side by side, like two unsteady fireflies.

"It's a little spooky, isn't it?" said Oliver. "Don't you think it's spooky, Randy?"

"Of course not," scoffed Randy. "Just these same old woods and this same old road."

When they had parked their bicycles at the roadside, though, she felt less confidence. It *was* spooky. The woods were so dark; moon-spangled only here and there, and the dead leaves made such a rustle as they walked. For some reason one does not like to make so much commotion in the woods at night.

Their flashlights were a help, sending beams along familiar vistas. Once they were frozen by the sight of two lighted amber eyes confronting them, but it turned out to be just somebody's house cat out hunting. Still, their steps quickened after that, and soon they were climbing the long hill on the other side of which the cave was hidden.

It was indeed a hidden cave, for when at last one descended to the sandstone ledge on the other side it was not to be seen. It lay concealed behind a wall of junipers and to reach it one must push one's way through this scratchy thicket.

First, though, the children paused on the shelf of stone and looked out at the moonlit view; wooded hills and then more wooded hills, and not a house in sight.

"What if we were the only people?" said Randy. "Just you and I and no one else. And no towns or cars or railroad trains or churches. Just more and more of that." She waved her hand at the sleeping hills.

"We're not the only people, though," said Oliver stoutly. He did not wish to be alarmed uselessly. "The Steinkraus's farm is over there and Mr. Cutmold's house is over that way. It's just that you can't see them."

"But *if* we were," said Randy. "If we were pre-historic, then, pretend, and this region was alive with dinosaurs, and the cave had pterodactyls in it!"

"Oh, Randy," said Oliver, who was going to grow up to be a scientist, "I should think you'd know by this time that people weren't invented then. Only reptiles, all kinds, but no *people!* They didn't begin till millions of years later, when all the dinosaurs were dead."

"Saber-toothed tigers, then," persisted Randy. "Mammoths and things like that. People were alive when those were. Suppose we found a saber-toothed tiger in that cave?"

"I'd kill him with Rush's scout knife," said Oliver, who had prudently armed himself with this weapon.

"You couldn't, you wouldn't have a knife; you'd be a prehistoric savage."

"Then I would have thought up how to make a slingshot," said Oliver. "I'd kill him with that. Now come *on*, Randy, let's go in. You go first; you're a girl."

Randy ardently desired not to go in first. "In cases of this kind the boy goes first," she said, and after a short earnest argument they reached a compromise and side by side, rather squeezed together, plunged through the scratchy juniper screen.

Their flashlights illuminated the familiar cave, and there was nothing there to scare them: no saber-toothed tiger or leather-winged pterodactyl; just a couple of old Pepsi-Cola bottles left there by Rush and Mark, and a forgotten baseball cap that had been chewed by crickets.

Their shadows were enormous on the rough, curving walls.

"Now we must step—very carefully—to the right. One. Two. Three," said Randy. They turned their flashlights toward the ground but there was nothing there: just sandy floor and old chokecherry pits.

"Perhaps we should dig," suggested Oliver. He knelt down and scraped away at the sand with the point of the scout knife, but found nothing.

Randy flashed her light about the cave: floor, walls, ceiling; and then she screamed so piercingly that Oliver's hair stood up on end. (He noticed this in one corner of his mind, for he had always supposed it to be a figure of speech, not a possible fact.)

"Gosh, what's the matter?"

"The bats!" Randy was shrieking. "Look up at the

ceiling; they're all hung up there, slews of them! I thought they flew south in winter like the birds!"

It was true: great numbers of bats were hanging upside down from the ceiling like little black umbrellas; to Randy worse than any pterodactyl.

"They hibernate, silly," shouted Oliver, for Randy had precipitately left the cave. "They're fast asleep; they'd never hurt you, anyway. Come on back in."

But Randy had had enough. Oliver, being a boy and a scientist, knew a lot about bats and didn't mind them very much. He returned to the cave door and again stepped three paces to the right, knelt down and scraped at the sandy floor. This time no clue, but an old penny, came to light. A very old penny. There was an Indian's head on it, turned greenish with age, and its date was 1900. Oliver was very pleased.

"Gee whiz," he called. "I found a penny older than Father is!"

"Good luck!" called Randy. "But no clue?"

"No. I'll try again though in a minute. Now I'm going to eat my chocolate, to keep my strength up."

He tried several more times after that, taking first three small steps, then three very large ones, and finally just in case the clue writer had made a mistake, he tried three paces to the left. All without success.

"But what other cave is there?" said Randy as they pedaled home. "There's that crack in the rock back of our house, but you can't really call it a cave, and it hasn't anything to do with cake crumbs. Cake crumbs. Cave.

A cave well known to us. . . . Does it make you think of anything at all?"

"Only about that cave in "Tom Sawyer," and the piece of cake that he and Becky Thatcher ate when they were lost in it. But that's just a fictionary cave; it couldn't be the one."

"But it could be, I bet. Oh, Oliver, it *might* be in the pages of the book, don't you see? Somewhere in the cave chapter! Oliver Melendy," said Randy very earnestly, "you are much, much more intelligent than I am."

"Wait till we see if it's right. Where is the book, anyway?"

"In the Office, I think. I'm not sure."

John Doe growled from the kitchen when they came in, but they were able to reassure him before he barked. They crept up the stairs breathlessly, whispering to Isaac so that he'd know who they were and not bark, either.

In the Office the moonlight lay in bluish rectangles below the western windows, one rectangle bent and touching a part of the bookcase, but "Tom Sawyer" was not among the books that were silvered by its light.

"And of course it wouldn't be by this time," said Randy sensibly. "An hour ago it would have been shining over here, about. Or here. Yes, and *here's* the book, third from the left-hand corner!"

"The cave chapter's toward the back——"

"I know, and here's the clue—wait, I'll turn on

the light; yes, just where it should be, right next to the page about the cake——"

"What does it *say?*"

"Sh-h. Whisper. Come closer:

"Well loved by one, by all well known,
As black as jet, as white as bone,
    My voice, now silent, often soars;
    And I have keys for many doors.
Among these keys is one for you.
A.B.C. Unlock the clue."

"I don't get it," said Oliver.

"But I *do,*" said Randy, her eyes shining. And as Oliver watched, she walked straight over to Rush's battered upright piano and struck first the A key, then B, and last the key of middle C. Middle C gave a peculiar twang like a broken harp string, not at all its customary sound, and leaping onto the piano stool Randy lifted the lid of the old piano, reached down among the dusty strings and felts and drew out a blue paper; Oliver, meanwhile, hopping up and down in a dance of joy.

Before they could read that message it contained, however, they were interrupted by the appearance of Father and Cuffy, who came up the stairs in their bathrobes, much startled, to say the least.

"What in the *world*——" began Cuffy.

"Aha," said Father. "I sensed a mystery in all that early-to-bed performance. Now how about an explanation?"

Randy and Oliver had a hard time making their midnight activities sound reasonable or even plausible; and Cuffy was little or no help. "Not only playing the piano at one A.M., Mr. Melendy; but searching people's pockets, if you please, and looking for Chinese statues in the middle of the night; breaking china, spending days and days in graveyards. *I* don't know what ails them or what they're after. I declare. I do declare! Now they'll be no good at all in school tomorrow."

"Tomorrow night, children," said Father, "you will go to bed the minute you get home from school. Is that clearly understood?"

Yes, they understood that; and when he spoke so firmly they knew there was no use in pleading.

"Is it for punishment or for our health?" whispered Oliver as they went downstairs.

"Both, I guess," said Randy, "though he doesn't seem very cross. Not half as cross as Cuffy, and not half as surprised, either. Do you suppose he *knows?*"

"I think maybe he might," said Oliver.

A few minutes later Randy managed to slip into his room and read him the latest clue.

"Between two roofs and high and dry,
With dust and spiderwebs I lie,
And watch the winter creeping by.
　(But think of speed and summer breeze,
　Of winding roads and flashing trees,
　New fields to conquer. Think of these.)"

"Hmmm," said Oliver. "It must be in Carthage or Braxton or some other place where the houses are close together. How else could it be high up and between two roofs?"

"I think it's poorly worded," said Randy critically. "How in the world can it be high and dry if it's out in the open like that?"

"Maybe they've put it in a tin can or a bottle or something," said Oliver doubtfully.

"But goodness, there are hundreds of houses! We can't just go climbing up on all the roofs around here."

"Anyway," said Oliver, "we did all right tonight: two clues inside a minute, just about. Pretty good!"

"Yes, it's certainly a record. Oh, help, here comes Cuffy! Good night, sleep tight!"

Randy vanished down the hall.

CHAPTER XI

Between Two Roofs

Between two roofs and high and dry,
With dust and spiderwebs I lie,
And watch the winter creeping by.
   (But think of speed and summer breeze,
   Of winding roads and flashing trees,
   New fields to conquer. Think of these.)

SHORTLY AFTER the moonlight expedition, Oliver
came down with German measles.

"I wondered how long you were going to overlook

them," Cuffy said. "You've made a thorough investigation of everything else from chicken pox to mumps to croup. Cheer up though, my lamb, it's best to get it over with, and it won't last long."

She was right, as usual. After two uncomfortable days when he had a temperature, Oliver developed a fancy rash like red lace all over his stomach, and at once felt better. But it was boring to be in bed. Randy had had German measles long ago and was in school. Father was working in his study. Willy was building a new henhouse back of the stable. Cuffy was cleaning out the kitchen. Isaac was asleep on the floor near by, busily dreaming of chasing rabbits. Oliver was left to his own devices.

First he mounted some butterflies left over from last summer (and got the bed full of pins); then he took apart an old alarm clock but could not put it back together again so that it would run, and after that he painted some pictures of sky battles and bombs exploding and got water color on the sheets and pillow case; and then he ate a few cookies and read some old comic books that he had, and after that he just tossed about among the pins and crumbs and groaned with boredom.

Isaac's paws twitched, and he whimpered in his sleep. Oliver groaned and thought about the clue. They had got no place with it. I wonder if it could be up on our own roof, he thought. Well, maybe it could be. I mean suppose it was up on our roof and at the same time just under the edge of the *cupola* roof. That way it would be between two roofs. I bet that's it! Yes, but what about the winding roads and flashing trees, and all? Well, it could mean that from the roof you'd get a good *view* of trees and roads and stuff. And I bet there's lots of dust and spiderwebs up there. Yes, but what about speed, though, and summertime?

Still, in spite of these unanswered questions, he became more and more hopefully convinced that he had solved the riddle of Clue Eleven's hiding place.

"And I feel perfectly okay," he said to Isaac, who opened one eye skeptically and closed it again. "It's just this rash that doesn't itch much; and it wouldn't take me a minute, and I wouldn't make any noise."

I better *not* make any noise, he told himself as, a second later, barefooted and in his pajamas, he sped up the stairs to the Office and then up the little steep stairs to Mark's cupola room. The windows had not been opened in a long time and they all stuck in their cases, but finally Oliver got one open and stepped out on the flat top of the mansard roof.

It was wild and windy, a day late in March. The spruce trees swept their boughs against the house, and the sky was full of big, hurtling clouds, and crows blown off their courses.

"I hope they'd have the sense to anchor down the clue," said Oliver, "or it would have blown away long ago."

There were little swirls of dust on the roof, and even some old rags of last year's cobwebs up beneath the eaves; but there was no clue. There was nothing of interest. Oliver walked all around the cupola and then to the edge of the roof where he stood still, with his teeth chattering, looking north to Carthage, where, across the empty fields, great cloud shadows were hurrying. Cold and windy though it was, it was good to be outdoors again.

"OLIVER MELENDY!!" shouted a terrible voice, and Oliver looked down into the upturned face of Cuffy, her arms full of dish towels and her face full of outrage.

He scuttled into the house and downstairs to his bed to await his scolding. He got it, too, and for several days Cuffy watched him like a hawk to see if he developed complications, but he didn't, luckily, and by the time he was entirely recovered Easter vacation had begun, and Mona and Mark and Rush were all at home again.

Another nice thing was that Mrs. Oliphant came for a visit; she had paid them a number of visits since Christmas. Added to her other virtues she believed in presents, and always brought them something that they liked: a pair of Javanese puppets on one occasion, a handful of peacock feathers on another, and once an old-fashioned, pretty music box with one note missing that made the tune limp; it had been her own in her long-ago childhood. On this particular visit she brought a chocolate rabbit two feet high, wearing a straw hat and carrying a basket full of hard-boiled eggs. Nobody could bear to eat it except Oliver who surreptitiously nicked off an edge of paw or ear whenever he found himself alone with it.

Easter Sunday was a beautiful day, though windy. The crocuses that Mona had planted two years ago came up and blossomed just in time. "Like little Easter egg cups," Randy said. Mona made herself a new hat out of a spray of artificial lilac and some veiling from the dime store. She made one for Randy, too, using a piece of yellow ribbon, some cloth daisies, and one of Oliver's butterflies. Both were very pretty hats, but having been designed more for effect than for endurance the girls, while wearing them, moved their heads with extreme care as though they had stiff necks.

"Maybe I'll just give up acting and design hats when I grow up," said Mona, with pins in her mouth. "Honestly, Rush, look at us; don't we look fashionable?"

"Uh-hunh, pretty sharp," said Rush with mild enthusiasm; he hardly seemed to see the hats at all. But when, in all their finery, they went out to get into the Motor to go to church, the first thing they saw was Lorna Doone, the horse, greedily cropping crocuses on the front lawn, and on her head she, too, was wearing a new bonnet; a dashing creation made up of Cuffy's feather duster, some paper roses, and the family toothbrushes arranged in a cockade, all tastefully held in place with adhesive tape and the cord from somebody's pajamas.

"Rush, you scoundrel!" cried Mona, but she laughed as hard as everybody else.

"I think she looks kind of stylish, like a circus horse," said Mark. "When we come home, let's hitch her to the surrey and go for the first ride of the season."

The ride, however, was delayed; first by the large dinner they all ate, and then by the natural languor following upon the dinner, and then by the fact that the surrey had to be cleaned and dusted before they could use it. Rush even got up on a stool and swept off the roof with such vigorcus strokes that clouds of dust descended upon Randy, and also, unexpectedly, a little wad of paper: pale blue paper.

She stared at it for a moment before she realized what it was and pounced upon it, screaming.

"Between two roofs!" she yelped. *"On* the surrey roof and *under* the stable roof. Oh, but I don't think that was quite fair——" she stopped abruptly. Mark was staring at her; so was Rush.

"You nuts?" inquired her brothers kindly.

"No," said Randy. "It's just—it's just—oh, you wouldn't understand!" With that she fled from the stable, shouting for Oliver.

She found him astride one of the iron deer wearing his cowboy hat and reading the Sunday funnies which flapped and crackled in the breeze.

"Why didn't you answer me? Listen, I've got it!"

"Hm-m?" said Oliver. "Answer you? I was reading about this dumb character, a rabbit named Spoofy, and how he's having trouble with this other character, a

woodchuck——" (Oliver had caught the word "character" from Rush.)

"Oliver, listen! It's the *clue*, dope; I've got the
clue!"

"*Where?* Why didn't you say so?"

"It was on the surrey roof the whole time! Rush just
knocked it off by accident."

"But it said *between* two roofs, didn't it?"

"Yes, and so it was: on top of the surrey roof and
under the stable roof. See? Though it doesn't seem
just the right way to phrase it——"

"So that's what they meant by speed and winding
roads. What does this one say?"

"It's sort of stately. It says:

"Those which are broken, here achieve perfection,
    Those which are scattered, here become as one;
Splendid as jewels arranged for our inspection,
    Brilliant as dewdrops blazing in the sun,
        And in design as fleeting as the dew.
        Here, close to these bright changelings, find the
            clue."

"Gosh," said Oliver.

"I know," sighed Randy.

Instead of whooping and leaping as the occasion demanded, they crossed the lawn to the waiting surrey
with lagging steps and preoccupied faces, to take the
season's first ride.

Luckily, they soon forgot their cares. Lorna Doone enjoyed being in harness again and clip-clopped briskly along the country roads, her mane rippling and the sunlight flashing on her coronet of toothbrushes. And the weather was so lovely! It promised spring for the first time; and within the promise of spring lay the promise of summer, when the family would all be together like this for a long time, and make many, many such excursions.

CHAPTER XII

Bright Changelings

Those which are broken, here achieve perfection,
   Those which are scattered, here become as one;
Splendid as jewels arranged for our inspection,
   Brilliant as dewdrops blazing in the sun,
     And in design as fleeting as the dew.
     Here, close to these bright changelings, find the
     clue.

OLIVER WENT to pay a visit to Miss Bishop one Saturday afternoon. He had done so several times since
their first meeting, once accompanied by Randy and

Father, both of whom had liked her. This pleased Oliver, who had a proprietary air toward Miss Bishop, as though by meeting her first he had, in a way, invented her.

He liked her house. It was nice and full of objects that had stories attached to them, and Miss Bishop could unwind these narratives as tidily as she might unwind a ball of yarn. Like many a lonely person she loved to talk when she had the chance, and Oliver was glad to listen. He would sit on the rug among the cats while his hostess made pomander balls, or herb sachets, or mended. When the weather was right, as spring advanced, he would crawl along beside her in the garden helping with the weeding. (At home he never weeded unless prodded, but here it was different.)

This particular afternoon, however, was rainy. It had commenced to rain when he was halfway there, and he arrived at Miss Bishop's house soaking wet; he was forced to take refuge in one of her housecoats while his clothes were hung on the firescreen to dry. It was cozy in the little house: the fire hissed and snapped, and the rain sounded as if it were being flung in handfuls against the window. Miss Bishop had prepared a tray of tea and seed cookies and watercress sandwiches (made with wild brook watercress, not bought, and for this reason Oliver, who normally did not care any more for watercress than for weeding, gobbled them enthusiastically).

Aunt Belle had a new set of kittens, too; their eyes had opened only two days ago and were a blank grey-blue color. They had tiny upright tails, and the pads of their paws looked like little pink raspberries. Every now and then Oliver would scoop one up to hold against his cheek or just to marvel at: at the tiny triangle of nose, the thin, curved ears, the teeth, small and sharp as thorns. He felt happy and comfortable. He felt welcomed and appreciated, and planned to stay for several hours.

The failure to find the twelfth clue ceased, for a little while, to bother him. That they had definitely failed on this one he was sure. Never had they taken so long to trace their objective: already it was the middle of May and they had no idea of what to look for; they had worried and worked and racked their brains, but they simply could not understand the poem.

"All I can think of is that they mean a rainbow," Randy had groaned. "Those which are broken here achieve perfection," and "those which are scattered here become as one." Maybe they're talking about all of the trillions of raindrops in a rainbow."

"But those raindrops *don't* become as one," objected Oliver. "They only seem to because of the way the sunlight strikes them, and makes them look like a big arch standing still."

"Well, I don't know; these mysterious clue writers take liberties sometimes. 'Fleeting as dew' and 'splendid as jewels.' What else could they mean? But you can't get close to a rainbow. I know because I've tried; long ago when I believed in the pot of gold I tried, and you just *can't.*"

"Oh, everybody's tried," said Oliver. "I don't think they're talking about a rainbow at all. Anyway how could they be sure there was going to *be* a rainbow? Maybe there won't be one around here for twenty years, for all they know."

"Yes, I suppose that's a point," Randy conceded. "Oh dear."

They were really stymied.

But today they had stopped worrying for a while. Randy and Pearl Cotton and Daphne Addison had all gone to Braxton to a long, luxurious double-feature movie, and Oliver was here, draped in Miss Bishop's housecoat, drinking tea. (Weak, with cream and three lumps of sugar, the way he liked it. Rush called it an "orange-pekoe milkshake.")

"That's a very pretty thing you're making, Miss Bishop," remarked Oliver politely.

She held up her crocheting so he could see it better. Another mat, he supposed. Miss Bishop was addicted to mats; she put them everywhere, on things and under things and over things.

"I invented this pattern myself," she said, with some pride. "I call it the snowflake. See, it has six sides."

"Why it does look like one, sort of," Oliver agreed.

"I've always been partial to snowflakes," said Miss Bishop. "Ever since I was a child. I can still remember the day I discovered they weren't just little dabs of white, just little frosty feathers coming down. I was seven years old, and I had a brand-new winter coat; navy blue. I wore it to church—it was too big for me, they always bought my clothes too big for me so I could grow into them, but by the time the clothes fitted me just right they were handed down to my little sister Ethel so *she* could grow into them, and by the time they fitted *her* just right they were ready for the rag bag. . . . Let's see, where was I?"

"You had this new coat," Oliver said.

"Oh, yes. Big though it was, it was new and I was proud of it. Well, coming home from church that day it started to snow. Fine, dry flakes. I looked at one on my new navy blue sleeve and all at once I felt that I had discovered something breath-taking! Something tremendous, like the law of gravity or the existence of the solar system! I stood right there where I was and I shouted. '*Papa!*' I shouted. 'The snow is made of little stars! It's not just snow; it's all little teeny weeny kinds of stars!' Papa didn't seem a bit excited. 'Yes, Lou,' he said. 'They're crystals. The raindrops freeze and crystallize in geometric patterns. That's why they look that way.' But I was just beside myself, I never had seen anything so pretty! When I got home I borrowed my grandma's reading glass and sat on the front stoop examining the perfect little things, and I saw that there were many varieties of the six-sided pattern. I wanted to do something about them; keep them, hold onto them some way, and I thought maybe if I drew pictures of them I would at least have a memory of the way they looked—really, I must have been a little crazy with excitement—so I went and got a pad and pencil and commenced to work——"

"You must have been an awful good drawer," Oliver said.

"That was just it. Of course I wasn't. I was only seven years old, untalented and slow; and in my effort I kept leaning too close and breathing hard on the crystals so that before I even got the second line on paper the snowflake I'd be drawing would just sort of dim out and fade away to water. I was frantic, but I kept on trying and always failing till at last, what with frustration and haste and rage at my own clumsiness, I began to cry. I howled. I opened my mouth and simply howled.

"Well, past the fence just then came Mr. Lansdorf. He was a German gentleman, the grandfather of my best friend, Augusta Schrader; he'd come over for a long visit with his daughter, Augusta's mother, and everyone had grown to love him. He was generous and jolly, and he had such rosy cheeks and such a lovely curly white beard that when he played the part of Santa Claus at the church Christmas festival he needed no disguise except the costume."

"Sort of like Mr. Titus with a beard," said Oliver.

"Yes, and with a strong German accent. When he saw me (and heard me) he said, 'Vy are you with such a big open mouth crying, little Lou?' And I howled sadly,

'It's the snowflakes. They don't last long enough, and they're so beautiful.' 'Vy you vish they should a long time last?' he said. 'Always there are more coming.'

" 'I want to draw them,' I explained. 'I want to draw all the different kinds so I'll remember them.'

" 'So. Then you vill drawing be until time ends, little Lou,' he said. 'Because each flake is different from each other flake, no two are matching, and see there are from the sky coming so many of them! So many, many hundreds every time it snows!'

"He opened the gate and came in and sat down beside me looking more like Santa Claus than ever with the snow sparkling in his beard and on his tufty eyebrows. He wore a fur cap, too; in those days men often did, and it was wonderfully becoming. I wiped away my tears, and together we watched the snowflakes through Grandma's glass, and it was true, just as Mr. Lansdorf said, no two were exactly alike.

"Not long after that he went home to Germany, and in the spring a present came to me from him. There was a note with it that said, 'For little Lou. These crystals will not melt away, though like the flakes of snow each design is different.' And in the box there was a big kaleidoscope, the first one I'd seen and the best one I ever did see. Wait a minute, I still have it. I'll show it to you."

A log crumbled in the fire, Aunt Belle purred among her kittens, the rain tapped at the window. In a moment Miss Bishop returned with the kaleidoscope; a large stout one bound in worn red leather that gave evidence of great use, but when Oliver held it up to the light and peered into it with one eye, he saw that the colorful and complicated patterns within it were as perfect and as bright as new.

"We have one of these at home," he said. "A good one, too, but not as good as this. This one's neat! Brother! Here's a design that looks like the splendidest crown you ever saw!"

Very carefully so as not to jar the pattern, Oliver handed the cylinder to Miss Bishop who looked into it, expressed admiration, then turned it a few times herself until she saw a design that made her think of Ali Baba's treasure, and then she carefully handed it back to Oliver.

"Isn't it wonderful?" she said. "All these changing designs, each one different, each one perfect, and all made with a couple of mirrors and a jumble of broken glass! Just chips of colored glass, Oliver, and in the kaleidoscope they look like jewels."

"Like jewels," repeated Oliver in a queer voice. He put the kaleidoscope down on his knee and sat staring at Miss Bishop.

"Why, Oliver, what is it? Do you feel all right?"

"Miss Bishop, I'm awful sorry, but I have to go home. What you said just reminded me about something. Something I have to do right away. I'm awfully sorry."

"But, honey, it's still raining!"

"Oh, that's all right, I'll run fast!"

In the end he reluctantly agreed to borrow a rain-coat and ran flapping like a flounder down the road, with pink plastic billowing around him.

"Hi there," said Willy Sloper who was coming out of the house just as Oliver flapped in. "What are you impersonating? Bubble gum?"

"Where's Randy?" croaked Oliver breathlessly.

"Still over to Braxton to the pictures, I guess," said Willy.

"Heck, and it's a double feature," groaned Oliver, who, since he was honorable, knew he would have to wait for his sister before he seized the clue.

When, a little after six, he heard the Cottons' car in the driveway, he flew to the door. Randy took forever to say good-bye. Hovering there impatiently he could hear feminine giggles and cackles issuing from the car and at last was goaded into shouting, "Hey! Hurry up!"

Then she came. "Well, goodness, what's the rush?"

"I know where the clue is!"

"No! Honestly? Oh, *where?*"

"Follow me."

"Not in the Office again!" exclaimed Randy as they started up the second flight of stairs.

"Yup. I'm sure of it. Wait'll you see!"

After a short fierce search by Oliver, the kaleido-scope was located at the very bottom of the toy box.

"Of *course!*" cried Randy. "The broken things and the jewels and all! But how did you ever guess it?"

"Tell you in a minute," said Oliver. "Here, help me get the thing out, will you? It's there all right, but it's way down inside."

They managed to snake out the little roll of blue paper with a pencil, and Randy read the rhyme as usual:

"A heart is cold that once was hot.
    A voice is still that once was bold.
Seek in the dust of flames forgot
    For that which you would seize and hold!"

"Oh, now honestly," said Randy. " 'Flames forgot.' For goodness sake, what kind of talk is that? I suppose they must mean ashes of some sort, but nothing poetic rhymes with ashes—mashes, splashes, crashes——"

"Measle rashes," contributed Oliver.

"Mustaches," added Randy. "So they have to talk about 'the dust of flames forgot' instead."

"If they're talking about ashes they must mean to look in the fireplaces then, don't you think?"

"It sounds that way. But Father's still using his. Gee whiz, I hope it hasn't been burned up!"

"Oh, I guess they wouldn't take any chances. Let's go down and have a look."

"Ran-dee? Oli-ver?" called Cuffy's voice relentlessly. "Time to set the table now and get ready for your supper!"

"Heck," said Oliver. "Some meal is always interfering."

"First time I ever heard you speak unkindly of a meal," said Randy. "Never mind, though, we'll go to work tomorrow. Now tell me, how did you ever guess about the kaleidoscope!"

CHAPTER XIII

Seek in the Dust

A heart is cold that once was hot.
    A voice is still that once was bold.
Seek in the dust of flames forgot
    For that which you would seize and hold!

BUT ON the next day there was a rude shock in store
for them: Willy, since it was springtime and warm,
had cleaned out all the fireplaces. Where, until yesterday, there had been soft beds of ash, there was now nothing but clean brick and fans made out of newspaper between the andirons.

"But they must have known this might happen,"

said Randy. "They would have warned us, I'm sure they would have. They warned us about the ice cube, and told us the time was limited."

"Maybe they thought we'd find it earlier, though; the way they thought we'd find the Kwan Yin clue later than we did."

"Perhaps it's not even *in* a fireplace," Randy said. "Those ashes would be an awfully chancy hiding place, anyway. Do you think they might have put it in the chimney?"

A great light of anticipation broke on Oliver's face. "Ever since Cuffy read me Water Babies, when I was seven, I've wanted to be a chimney sweep like Tom. Or at least to try it out! And now I can!"

Randy looked doubtful. "Gosh, I don't know. Suppose you got stuck?"

"Oh, I wouldn't," said Oliver, and would have started up the chimney immediately if Randy hadn't urged him to go and put on his oldest clothes.

"Sneakers, too," she called, as he ran upstairs. "It might be sort of slippery."

Boys enjoy the queerest things, she thought. *I* wouldn't want this job.

Since the living-room fireplace was the largest one they decided that was the place to start from. Randy crept in with Oliver, gave him a boost, and somewhere up above the damper he got a fingerhold and then a toehold and began his cautious climb. Soot fell in showers upon Randy who leaped aside, anxiously clasping her smudged hands together.

"Are you all right?" she called.

There were grunts of effort and sounds of scraping and scratching within the chimney. More soot fell.

"I don't think the clue's up here," said Oliver in a muffled, miserable voice. "I don't think anybody's ever been up here before. The soot is thick and it looks like fur, but it's not *attached;* it comes off if you breathe on it, even, and I've got it in my eyes and up my nose, and I don't like it!"

"Come on down then," urged Randy, alarmed at the black avalanches descending from the chimney.

There were more sounds of struggle in the flue and some chips of mortar hurtled down. "I can't," said Oliver at last. "I'm stuck. My belt is caught on something and I can't reach my arm around to unhitch it."

"Try to wiggle up off of it," advised Randy.

More frantic scratchings, more soot, more (and larger) lumps of mortar. "It doesn't work," reported Oliver in a worried voice. "I'm just as stuck as ever."

"Wait, I'll get Willy, he's tall, he can reach you," said Randy. "Don't worry, Oliver, just stay where you are."

"Where did you think I'd be going?" inquired Oliver crossly. He really was very unhappy. It was so dark and lonesome where he was, and it smelled dismally of old dead ancient smoke. Suppose Willy failed to unhitch him? Suppose nobody could get him out? They'd have to leave him there forever and lower his food down on a pulley line, or else they might have to take the chimney apart, perhaps tear down the house, which would be inconvenient, untidy and expensive, and Father and Cuffy would be upset. Oliver sniffled, and a tear tracked down his sooty cheek. He could hear John Doe barking spiritedly out of doors somewhere, and Cuffy singing in the kitchen; but it was as though they were in a far-off, unattainable world. A sound of sobbing issued from the flue.

"Here now, here now," said Willy's reassuring voice. "Don't you be crying none, we'll get you out in just a jiffy; and you don't want Cuffy comin' in and gettin' all excited, do you now?"

Oliver gulped lugubriously and waited as Willy, prudently wearing a raincoat, got into the fireplace, stood up on a footstool, and reached his long arm upward between Oliver and the old black bricks, located the snared belt and freed it. Then he got out of the way and Oliver came down onto the hearth with a thud, looking nothing in the world like Santa Claus.

"Man, are you a mess!" said Randy, in a tone of wonder. "You remind me of the Tar Baby. Willy, what can we ever do with him?"

Willy considered. "Best thing, I guess, is to arrange for him to fall into the brook clothes and all. Good thing it's a warm day. And better fall in with a cake of soap while you're at it; you go get one, Randy, and I'll carry him to the front door or he'll leave a set of foot-prints no one could overlook!"

When Randy returned with the soap she found Willy waiting at the front door; across the lawn, black as a golliwogg, Oliver was running toward the brook.

"You better make use of that soap yourself, too, Randy," Willy said. "Your face don't look too good; it's kind of striped. And while you're gettin' rid of the evidence outdoors I'll be gettin' rid of it in here."

"Willy darling, you're a hero! You're a saint!"

"Just one thing," said Willy plaintively. "Why, Randy, *why* do you kids do things like climbin' up chimney flues?"

"We'll tell you soon, Willy, really we will. We're not crazy. Oh, and Willy, when you took the ashes out of the fireplaces did you happen to notice if there was a piece of blue paper? With writing on it?"

"Oh, no! Not again!" groaned poor Willy. "Always these pieces of paper with writin' on 'em! You kids have got a—a—an *ob*-session about pieces of blue paper! No, I didn't see none."

Later, when they were clean and dry once more, Randy had another idea.

"Do you suppose they mean the chimney of Mark's deserted house?" she suggested.

"Why, I was thinking of the same thing!" said Oliver.

"We'll go there Saturday and see," said Randy. "We'll take our lunch and spend the day."

It was a wonderful May morning when they set out. All over the countryside the orchards were in bloom, and petals speckled the breeze like pink and white confetti. Everywhere there was the new, new green of spring, and the fields were dappled with the yellow of wild mustard and buttercups and dandelions.

"It's funny how happy weather can make you," said Randy, as they sailed along the road on their bikes.

"Good weather like this can," said Oliver judiciously. "Brother, am I glad of spring! Billy Anton and me are building a wigwam, and we're going to sleep out in it when it gets warmer."

"Billy Anton and *I*," corrected Randy absently. "I wonder if I'll be able to get into my last-summer's dresses."

At the customary spot they parked their bicycles among the bushes at the roadside and walked into the woods. Birds were singing everywhere, and the ground was patterned with Dutchman's breeches and trillium and bloodroot.

"Spring flowers are white in the woods and yellow in the meadows," said Randy. "I wonder why? And then they're purple in the ditches where the violets grow."

Mark's deserted house wasn't really a house any more. It was only a lot of old stones in the underbrush and one tall chimney with a fireplace in it. Near the chimney grew a tall neglected lilac bush, now in bloom, and beyond stood the remnants of an apple orchard, also blooming. "Look, there's a new oriole's nest in one of the trees," said Oliver.

"A pocketful of gold," quoted Randy reminiscently. "Gee whiz, we've come a long way in the search since then, haven't we?"

"Thirteen clues!" said Oliver. "Come on, let's find the next one."

But poking in the old fireplace among the ashes of past picnic fires they found no scrap of blue, and the chimney overhead was noisy with the indignant chimney swifts who had their nests there.

"Well, heck, it isn't here," said Oliver. "So let's eat lunch."

"Are you kidding? I bet it isn't half past ten! Let's go and see what's happened to the well."

The well was as old as the house, deep, with an eye of water at the bottom that looked back at them. Its sides were covered with moss and tiny ferns. "And look," said Randy. "There are violets growing where the gentians bloom in the fall."

Oliver leaned over gingerly. He had once fallen into that well, and had treated it respectfully ever since. He dropped a pebble down into the pool, though, and so did Randy, for it was a custom they always observed, and besides it made a lovely sound.

Then they went wandering for a while. Lilies of the valley, gone wild, grew thickly all around the ruin and back into the woods. Randy picked a huge bunch of them, sniffing in their fragrance so heartily and often that it made her dizzy. The sun grew warmer on her stooping back, and Oliver from high up in an apple tree called, "Gee, it must be *nearly* lunchtime."

On the way home that afternoon Randy said, "We've looked in all the fireplaces that have anything to do with *us,* and I don't think it's in anybody else's, do you? The poem would have given a hint."

Oliver only yawned. The air and food and sunshine had been too much for him.

"But I know one place we haven't tried," continued Randy. "And I intend to look there as soon as we get home."

Oliver, too drugged by spring even to express curiosity, pedaled on in silence at her side.

Once home, though, he revived a little. "Okay, where is it, then?" he said, languidly letting his bicycle crash to the ground.

"Come," said Randy, mysterious and commanding.

"Oh boy, I think I get it!" said Oliver a moment later as she led him down the cellar steps.

It was cool in the cellar and smelled of cement; the light down there was dim and green, for the low windows were overgrown, now, with vines and leaves.

"Switch on the light," commanded Randy. Then she opened the door of the cold and silent furnace and stuck her hand inside. "Eureka!" she shouted, with a loud, metallic echo, for there at the bottom of the

furnace, with a sparse scattering of ashes and one forgotten clinker, lay the clue!

"Honest? No kidding?" yelped Oliver, no longer
sleepy. "Here, come out and let me see!"

Randy backed out of the furnace and held up the
blue paper.

"Read it! Read it!"

"Listen," said Randy. "Oliver! It's the last one!
Next we're to look for the reward itself!"

"Well, read it! I can't wait!"

"Okay.

"On the eleventh day of June,
At three o'clock that afternoon,
   (Not half past three or ten to four)
   Set out to seek a friendly door.
(A door unknown, a door that's new!)
First, follow Highway 22,
   Proceed, and take the next turn right,
   Beyond the cows of Herman Heidt.
Travel a mile and you will see
A Northern name, and a tall tree.
   Onward a little, round a bend,
   Behold the goal! Here's journey's end!"

"Now this one really gives good directions," said
Oliver approvingly. "Telling about cows and Highway
22, and turning right and all. Now if the other clues
had just been like that——"

"Oh, I'm glad they weren't," said Randy. "I liked all the adventures and mistakes and the crazy ways we found them in the end. But how, oh, Oliver, how are we going to *live* until the eleventh of June?"

CHAPTER XIV

A Door Unknown

On the eleventh day of June,
At three o'clock that afternoon,
   (Not half past three or ten to four)
   Set out to seek a friendly door.
(A door unknown, a door that's new!)
First, follow Highway 22,
   Proceed, and take the next turn right,
   Beyond the cows of Herman Heidt.
Travel a mile and you will see
A Northern name, and a tall tree.

Onward a little, round a bend,
Behold the goal! Here's journey's end!

FORTUNATELY THEY did manage to live, and the day,
when it arrived, was magnificent: June at its very
best, and nothing can be better than that. Everything
is on its way but not quite there: every flower, every
vegetable, every blade. Every nest is finished, and one
is just beginning to find those turquoise halves of robin's
eggs all over the place. The birds are still so noisy and
joyful that nobody can sleep late in the morning. Luckily not many people want to at this time of year. The
peonies are big as lettuces, the poppies, though rumpled,
are wide open, and in every garden in the world someone
is stooped over, gladly working.

In school, it was hard for the children to keep their
minds on study; through the open windows came such
warm gusts of air, such smells of flowers and new-cut
grass, such summer sounds of bee and bird and lawn
mower and airplane purring in the depthless sky! But
of all the absent-minded children in school that day
Randy Melendy and her young brother Oliver were the
worst.

"Dreaming again," said Miss Kipkin severely to
Randy. "The subject we are discussing, dear, is the Holy
Roman Empire, not the *Roman* Empire. There's a dif-
ference."

"There are not, and never have been, and never

will be three l's on the end of the word shall!" said Miss McMorrow severely to Oliver.

But at last, at last, the ordeal was over! They were set free at three o'clock, and flew to their bicycles without a backward glance.

They sped through the village waving at friends, shouting greetings, but never pausing for an instant. Soon the little town lay behind them and they were winging their way along Route 22.

"I never expected to have my heart start beating double time at the sight of Herman Heidt's repulsive cows, did you?" said Randy.

Oliver considered. "I don't think my heart's beating any oftener than it usually does," he said. "I sure feel interested though!"

"Just think, Oliver, the end! The *end* of months of search and toil! I'm almost scared."

"Why, I thought it was more like fun than toil. And I don't feel scared, either. I feel good."

"Oh, Oliver you're so *normal,*" objected Randy. "You're so normal that you're unique."

"Watch it, you almost missed the turn!" cried Oliver, and they scooped to the right and found themselves on a country road with wild hedges flanking it. Beyond the hedges lay the broad, peaceful landscape: softly colored fields, woods, distant hills. Swallows dipped through the air, and many white and yellow butterflies sailed upon it.

"There's a name on a mailbox, but all it says is Peltmayer. Would you call Peltmayer a Northern name?" said Oliver.

"Well, I don't *think* so," said Randy. "And it hasn't been a mile yet." After a moment or two she added, "I *hope* it isn't Peltmayer."

A little farther on there were woods edging the road, and they went coasting through a green tunnel. At the end of it, under an enormous sycamore tree, they saw a sign with blue letters.

"Villa Borealis!" Randy read aloud.

"That means Northern!" Oliver cried. "I remember from my star book: Corona Borealis means Northern crown, Aurora Borealis means Northern lights! Villa Borealis must mean Northern villa!"

"Elementary, my dear Watson," agreed Randy, in a voice that trembled slightly with excitement; for now they were pedaling along a winding drive and soon, at any instant, they would see their goal!

"I don't remember that there was any house here before, do you?" she said.

"Maybe it's a new one," said Oliver. "The road looks pretty new and kind of rough still, doesn't it?"

"Yes. But whose can it possibly be?"

Presently, rounding a bend, they came out into an open space, and then they saw that Oliver's deduction was correct. There, among birch trees, stood a brand-new house: new in every way, including style, for it was a modern house, low-lying yet spacious, warm in color, almost golden. It seemed to belong to the land on which it stood far more than houses usually do.

"This isn't what I expected at all!" said Randy half indignantly. "I imagined something kind of fairy-taleish and old-fashioned, I guess: a cottage rather like Miss Bishop's, with shutters and vines and a doormat saying 'Welcome.' "

"I saw it sort of like a castle," Oliver admitted.

"There's not a soul in sight," said Randy. "It looks deserted. Now don't you feel just a little bit scared?"

"I don't, but my stomach does," said Oliver.

Hesitantly they crossed a terrace to the door. At their left they saw, beyond a great glass panel, an empty room; a lovely room, with soft colors, and a wonderful fireplace, and bowls of flowering branches.

"That Chinese screen looks familiar," whispered Randy. "Haven't we seen one like it somewhere?"

"Maybe they make them all the same," said Oliver ignorantly. "Hurry up and ring the bell."

Randy rang it, and they stood there waiting. Their hearts were in their mouths. Nobody crossed the room beyond the glass panel, but somewhere else within the house they heard footsteps approaching. And was there a voice saying "Sh-h"? And was there a smothered giggle? Were they imagining things? Though he was a big boy, Oliver suddenly put his hand in Randy's.

The footsteps came closer. The door opened. Mrs. Oliphant opened it.

They stood rooted to the spot.

Mrs. Oliphant smiled at them demurely. "Welcome," she said. "Welcome to my new house, children, and won't you please come in?"

"But what—but how—I don't *understand*, Mrs. Oliphant," cried Randy. "Why didn't we know?"

"Because I wanted to surprise you," she said. "Come in, come in, and see how nice and new it smells! When you get to be as old as I am, you're apt to long for something new: a new viewpoint, a new idea! This house has both. . . . One carries so much age in oneself that it's all one needs of oldness; except old friends, of course. And if one has *young* old friends, so much the better," she added, patting their shoulders.

"This is the nicest thing I could have hoped for!" said Randy fervently.

"Brother, you can say that again!" Oliver agreed elegantly.

"And what a beautiful perfect house!" cried Randy. "Will you live in it all year round?"

"All year round," said Mrs. Oliphant. "I have had all I want of cities. I want a big piece of sky over my head for the rest of my life. In summertime I want to be kept awake by crickets instead of by taxi horns!"

"And we can come and see you all the time, and have meals here and things," said Oliver happily.

"Every day, if you wish," said Mrs. Oliphant.

Randy and Oliver were so full of delight and questions, and Mrs. Oliphant was so full of delight and explanations that it took some time to explore the lovely little house. The living room was as charming inside as it had looked from out of doors, and so were the other two rooms, each one of which, as Mrs. Oliphant had said, smelled radiantly new.

"The kitchen is my joy," she told them. "You just press a button or two and bells ring, lights flash on, and presto! An entire meal is cooked!"

The kitchen was Oliver's joy, too. He was particularly drawn to the electric dishwasher and a special device in the sink drain which had the distinction of being able to chew and swallow garbage. He foresaw many happy hours feeding the garbage-chewer and trying out the other gadgets, and was only reluctantly pried away now.

"But you must see my garden. Or at least what will be my garden someday," Mrs. Oliphant said. She led them through an open door at the back of the house out into the dazzling sunshine. "I have something better than flowers in it now!"

On the terrace three people were standing in a row: Mona and Rush and Mark!

Randy and Oliver could not believe their eyes; but hugs are easier to believe, and in less than a second they were being violently hugged, and hugging back!

"But how?" cried Randy. "I thought your schools got out at different times?"

"Within three days of each other," Mona said. "And Father fixed it so we could all surprise you together."

They saw now that Father was there, too, sitting on a low stone wall, beaming at them. Even the dogs were there, barking and jumping, sharing in the glorious excitement.

"Did *Father* know about the search?" asked Oliver.

"Of course; we all did," said Rush. "We all worked together, because we thought the winter might be tough for you with us away. Mrs. Oliphant and Father wrote the poems (it was Mrs. Oliphant's handwriting, by the way), and Mark and Mona and I thought up a lot of the places."

"Some places!" said Oliver, as he remembered the pokeweed forest; the capsule on Isaac's collar; the terrible Mr. Frederick.

"Did Cuffy and Willy know, too?" demanded Randy.

"Not till today. We couldn't tell them. They're so softhearted; we were afraid that if they saw you were discouraged they'd give you hints——"

"And we wanted to be sure you *worked*," said Mona virtuously.

"We were smarter than you thought we'd be," boasted Oliver. "We found the Kwan Yin clue long before Christmas, when you planned for us to find it; before Thanksgiving, even!"

"Yes, and at that it wasn't on the Kwan Yin; by mistake it had been put in one of Father's books," said Randy.

"No! It had? How come?" Mona and Rush and

Mark were startled, and Oliver and Randy explained; and after that all the adventures which had accompanied the search must be described. The voices rang out, laughed, interrupted, argued, in the good old Melendy way, and Mrs. Oliphant and Father listened and enjoyed.

"*Who* thought of Mr. Titus's alarm-clock bell?"

"Oh, Rush, of course, who else?"

"I *knew* it was Rush!" squealed Randy.

"What about the lichen in the graveyard?" said Oliver.

"Mark did that one," said Mona. "And the oriole's nest, too. He did all the sort of natural-history ones. Rush thought of Isaac's collar capsule, and I thought up the piano and the Kwan Yin."

"I thought up the ice cube," said Father unexpectedly; rather boastfully, too. "And the climbing boot, too. I thought you'd *never* find it. I had to go into all that long routine about looking for my other boots before you guessed it."

"*I* thought they'd never find the one on the surrey," said Rush. "Gosh, I had to *throw* it at Randy or they'd be looking for it still!"

"But on the whole you did remarkably well," Father told them. "We were sure we'd have to drop many more extra hints than we did."

"*We* thought we were superb," said Randy modestly. "Now who did the Tom Sawyer clue? Rush, I bet!"

"No, that was Father again," said Mona. "He thought of it when he was reading the book to you early in the winter, and we planned it at Christmastime."

"Mrs. Oliphant was responsible for the kaleidoscope and the furnace," Father said. "We all shared in it pretty equally, as you can see."

"Well, it was marvelous! It was perfect!" said Randy.

"Brother, you can say that again!" said Oliver.

"And now we are going to have a party," announced Mrs. Oliphant. "Here come Cuffy and Willy to help me get things ready."

"We'll all help," Randy volunteered, and Oliver said he would be glad to take charge of any garbage disposal that might be required.

It really was a party! As evening came on the cars began to arrive; and who should get out of them but all the people the Melendys liked best: Mr. Titus, Mr. and Mrs. Wheelwright, the Addisons, the Cottons, Miss Bishop, Billy Anton, Mr. Coughing and many others. After a wonderful huge picnic on the lawn (Mr. Titus arrived with seven pies and Mrs. Wheelwright with five dozen jelly doughnuts), everyone lay and gasped for a while and then played games in the fragrant summer dusk.

When it was really dark they went into the house and Rush played dance music on Mrs. Oliphant's piano and everybody danced. Everybody: Cuffy with Mr. Titus, Mrs. Oliphant with Father, Miss Bishop with

Mr. Coughing, Mona with Willy Sloper. Oliver could not bring himself to dance with a girl, so he danced with Isaac, who did not enjoy it.

Randy, alone, twirled and pirouetted through the open door and out onto Mrs. Oliphant's new lawn. The house with its glass panels was like a lighted lantern, festive and glowing. Music came from it and the babble of people enjoying themselves. What a lovely party! What a perfect night! Randy foresaw a long happy summer with constant journeyings to and fro between the new Villa Borealis and the old Four-Story Mistake.

"Randy?" It was Father calling her; she ran across the dewy grass to meet him.

"We're going to do a reel, and we need you," he said.

Randy slipped her arm through his. "This certainly was the 'rare reward' that the clue promised us," she said. "This day and night of wonderful surprises."

In the house two long lines of people were forming for the dance. Rush was skipping over the bars of "Turkey in the Straw."

"Be my partner, Randy, will you?" begged Oliver, anxiously. "I don't think Isaac could do the Virginia Reel."

"I certainly will!" said Randy warmly. "As partners you and I make a terrific team! Don't you think so?"

Oliver shoved his fat, tough-feeling little hand in hers as the music began in earnest.

"I think we do pretty good," he said.